Better Alive Than Dead:

Thirteen Tales of Monster Horror

By Rob E. Boley

ISBN-10: 1-940078-39-3
ISBN-13: 978-1-940078-39-7

Some of the stories in this book have been previously published.

"All of the Above" was originally published in *Clackamas Literary Review*, 2011.

"Bump" was originally published in the *Dayton Daily News* as winner of Best in Show in the Antioch Writers' Workshop/Dayton Daily News Story Contest in 2012.

"The Cat and the Goldfish" was originally published in *A cappella Zoo*, Spring 2010, edited by Colin Meldrum.

"A Clown and a Dragon Walk Into a Bar" was originally published in *Horror: Odd and Bizarre* by Sirens Call Publications, edited by Gloria Bobrowicz.

"GAG" was originally published in *AMOK! Short Sharp Shocks Vol I* by April Moon Books, edited by Neil Baker.

"The Harm" was originally published in *Once Bitten – Never Die* by Wicked East Press, edited by Jessica A. Weiss.

"Hungry Like the Moon" was originally published in *Best New Werewolf Tales*, edited by Carolina Smart.

"Low Hanging Sun" was originally published by *iHorror.com*.

"The Stink of Animosity" was originally published in *Necrotic Tissue*, April 2011, edited by R. Scott McCoy.

Dedication

For Ma'am

ICIIMH

Also by Rob E. Boley

The Scary Tales Series

That Risen Snow, a Scary Tale of Snow White and Zombies

That Wicked Apple, a Scary Tale of Snow White and Even More Zombies

That Ravenous Moon, a Scary Tale of Red Riding Hood and Werewolves

That Malicious Storm, a Scary Tale of Beauty and the Phantom

That Merciless Truth, a Scary Tale of Goldilocks and the Mummy

That Crooked Mirror, a Scary Tale of Cinderella and the Invisible Man

That Rotten Puppet, a Scary Tale of the Frog Prince and Frankenstein's Monsters

Table of Contents

"Every creature is better alive than dead, men and moose and pine trees, and he who understands it aright will rather preserve life than destroy it."

— Henry David Thoreau

Introduction

When I look back on my childhood, I see an imaginative little boy who was both terrified of what might be lurking in the dark but also conversely fascinated by monsters. In first grade, I had a habit of bringing scary toy creatures for show-and-tell, so much so that my teacher started calling me *The Monster Man*. "Oh no," she'd say, "here comes the Monster Man. What does he have this week?"

No doubt my love for monsters bloomed on Saturday nights, when I'd stay up late to watch old black and white horror movies presented by Dayton's local t.v. host, Dr. Creep. I especially loved the old Universal Studios films featuring such creature creations as Frankenstein's Monster, the Mummy, Dracula, the Creature from the Black Lagoon, and my personal favorite, the Wolf Man. No surprise that my debut dark fantasy novels, *The Scary Tales* series, feature mash-ups of fairy tale characters and these same horror monsters.

As a child who was at first awkwardly skinny and then later awkwardly chubby, I didn't have an abundance of confidence. Anxiousness plagued me, and sure, sometimes horror books and movies scared me. But somehow, these stories empowered me too. On the one hand, horror heightened that sense that danger was always lurking beneath the calm surface, but it also offered the notion that monstrous strength could emerge from even the most unlikeliest of places.

I think that's why I loved the Wolf Man so much. As portrayed brilliantly by Lon Chaney Jr., Larry Talbot was a regular guy who carried this terrible beast inside him. That duality intrigued me and offered me a strange solace. No doubt that's also reflected in my undying love of Batman, my favorite superhero. Sure, the dark night threatens us, but the Dark Knight protects us.

As well, sensitive portrayals like Chaney's showed me that monsters deserve compassion. I often found myself cheering for the creature in those old monster flicks, sympathizing with the man-made freak who only wanted a companion, or rooting for the outsider who was persecuted for the crime of being different. As Thoreau puts it, *every creature is better alive than dead.*

For truly, the best monster fiction offers us an uncompromising reflection, both of our selves and our neighbors. It forces us to look beneath the surface and see the monsters hiding inside us all.

Hopefully some of these grand notions resonate in these thirteen short stories. Of course, you'll meet some familiar creatures such as zombies, demons, interdimensional gods, werewolves, vampires, and even zombie werewolves, but you'll also discover some of my own monster creations, such as the man who knows everything, a cursed hole, a heartsick moon, or the woman whose own body is haunted. Sometimes, though, you'll no doubt discover that the real monsters are plain ole' humans.

I hope you also find plenty of thrills and chills, but also perhaps a bit of strength and inspiration . . . or even some compassion for these twisted dark souls.

Write on,
Rob "monstEr man" Boley

The Hygienist

The bell above the glass door chimes. The noise always makes her cringe. Catherine lets go of the door and steps into the standard climate of fake wood chairs and neat stacks of old magazines. The waiting room at Sunset Dental Services is every bit as empty as her heart. The night's cold breeze blows dead leaves ahead of her. The bell jingles again as the door closes behind her. The sound echoes in her empty heart, taking her back to the last time she saw her son, Connor. Maybe after tonight, she can end the pain once and for all. Maybe she'll be whole again.

The office smells vaguely of candy, the way watermelon gum tastes like watermelon, which is to say, not at all. She kicks the leaves aside and waves to the receptionist, Darlene, a cheerless crone with severe hair and yellowed teeth. Seems like she's always here, as much a fixture as the sign on the wall: *You don't have to brush all your teeth, only the ones you want to keep!"*

"Full moon tonight," Darlene says. On her dry lips, the words sound like an accusation.

Catherine nods. "Full house?"

Darlene stares at her through horn-rimmed frames. "I just hope we can make it through the night without an incident."

"We'll see, won't we? What time is the final patient?"

"4:15."

She sighs and pockets her keys—clutching them so they don't jingle. Through the next door, she walks down the hall. The doors to the restroom and the exam rooms are all open, but Doctor's private office remains shut. Typical. He hides from the patients until he absolutely has to face them. She can't blame him.

Catherine doesn't have an office. She's *only* a hygienist. She ducks into the bathroom and sits on the toilet.

The room smells of artificial lemons. She rummages in her purse, pulls out a silver flask, and swallows a generous belt of espresso-flavored vodka. She closes her eyes and savors the clean heat. It burns pure behind her breasts. She imagines white-hot flames gnawing at her empty heart. She licks her lips and pops a wad of gum into her mouth. Watermelon. Sure.

Her first patient is scheduled for 9 p.m. Doctor caters to a very particular clientele, the sort that keep late hours, pay well, and have special needs.

The bell above the door never chimes, but sure enough, Darlene offers her standard raspy greeting at 8:59.

"Good evening. Fill out this paperwork and our dental hygienist, Catherine, will be right with you."

A few minutes later, Catherine spits out her gum and walks down the hall. She opens the door to find a pale, blond-haired woman in the waiting room. She peers at Catherine over a well-worn issue of Entertainment Weekly. Brad Pitt grins from behind a peeling address label. The patient's wearing too much eyeliner.

"You must be Lisa," Catherine says.

The patient flashes a smile. "Yes, I absolutely must."

"Come on back. We'll be in Exam Room Two."

Catherine doesn't bother holding open the hallway door. Instead, she walks straight back to Exam Room Two. Sure enough, Lisa's already draped in the dental chair. Catherine ignores the theatrics. Such trickery no longer impresses her. It never did.

The room has no windows, though a set of venetian blinds hangs pointlessly on the outside-facing wall. A mural of cartoon sunshine with a wide smile is painted on the space behind the blinds, for the rare occasions when Doctor sees child patients. Right now, the blinds are closed.

Lisa arches an eyebrow at the blinds. "Am I your first victim of the night?"

"Hmm. You are."

"It's a full moon. I was surprised I was able to get an appointment."

"No, *they* tend to book the later appointments."

Catherine puts on her mask first, to hide her breath. She slides her hands—no longer shaking—into blue latex gloves. She learned the hard way that pink gloves make the patients aggressive. Blue is the least appetizing color, after all.

"Okay, open up."

Lisa opens wide, and Catherine can't help thinking of a bear trap. Her teeth gleam white. Her flawless skin might as well be airbrushed. Catherine resists the urge to run a blue finger down Lisa's sculpted cheek. She scrapes her probe at some plaque on the right mandibular central incisor but the night's final appointment weighs on her mind. Not thinking, she reaches for a dental mirror.

"That won't do you any good," Lisa says.

"I know. Sorry." She fumbles the mirror back onto the instrument tray.

"You sure you're ready for this? I can smell the *watermelon* on your breath."

"I'm fine."

Except she's not fine. Clearly. The patient—this night and what lies ahead—have her rattled. She accidentally makes eye contact with Lisa, a big mistake.

The patient's eyes are the color of marble, flecked with sunset pinks and ocean greens. Her pupils become endless holes that have their own gravity. Catherine's consciousness falls slowly inside that perfect darkness, a rapturous descent as sensuous as feathers over bare skin. Slices of frozen memories slide across her vision, like the photographs that ooze out of photo booths.

Her son walks alongside her through the nighttime woods. The leafless tree limbs shred the pale light from the bloated moon.

Metal jingles as her son hits the ground. The beast stares at her. Its yellow eyes gleam in the dark.

She runs after the monster that took her son. The leaves crunch under her feet. The beast howls in the distance, and she screams helplessly. Hot tears stream down her cheeks.

The images shatter. The darkness recedes.

Catherine's back in Exam Room Two's artificial light. She's sitting next to the patient on the exam chair. Lisa clutches her elbow, keeping her from falling.

Lisa has closed her eyes.

"Look away," she says, her voice now much deeper and distant.

The two words act like puppet strings, yanking Catherine's head to the side. She blinks and lets out what sounds like a stifled yawn. She takes a breath, and the patient pats her knee.

"You've lost someone," Lisa says, her voice back to normal.

Catherine can't look back, not yet. She tries to recall exactly how much the patient saw. The words come out of her, maybe something she heard in a movie or read in a book.

"It's like having a tooth ripped out," Catherine says, "except the roots never seem to heal. Everything's so fake now. Nothing feels real." She tips her head back and laughs. Not a pleasant sound. "And now I'm talking in bad rhyming poetry."

Lisa squeezes her hand, her grip cool and strong like a python. "You think you'll find him here? Would you even want to know him now?"

"He'd be about college-aged." She jerks her head, as if shaking free of the phantom puppet strings.

Enough of this. She won't sit here and have this thing fumble with her mind any longer. She retrieves the dental mirror from the floor—she doesn't remember it falling—and picks up instead the silver sickle-shaped scaler. The curve of its sharp hook gleams under the synthetic light.

"Okay, open up."

Lisa shrugs and opens her mouth. Her tongue lies flat and pink. She probably fed recently. Catherine presses her finger into the patient's mouth, adjusting her pretty lips to better see the molars.

"All the way, please."

The patient's upper lip curls into a snarl. Her four cuspid teeth, two on top and two below, slide out of the gum line like a cat flexing its claws. The four fangs each have a pink buildup of hard plaque around the gum line.

"You have to do a better job cleaning these," Catherine says, now scraping with her silver scaler. "Solenoglyph bacteria thrives below the gum line. This is a real problem for your kind."

The look on Lisa's face—wide eyes and furrowed brow—tells her that the patient has something to say. She retrieves her fingers from the open mouth.

"I've actually seen victims stare at the stains when I flick my teeth," Lisa says. "Their faces go from shock and horror to revulsion. I never wanted to be gross."

"You'll lose your fangs if you don't take care of them."

"It's hard when you can't see your reflection." It doesn't appear she's being defensive, just pointing out a fact.

"You do well enough with your makeup."

"Do I?" She half-smiles. "I worry that perhaps I go overboard with the eye liner."

Catherine chuckles. "You look great. At least you're not wearing that damned body glitter. That stuff gets everywhere. You wouldn't believe the places I've found it—sometimes days after a cleaning."

Lisa snarls. "Ever since those damn books came out."

The rest of the night is more of the same—a parade of freaks and creatures, some coming from as far as five states away. Doctor has a reputation among this community. By the end of the night, her feet throb. Her flask is near empty. The next to last patient just about slays her. Not even a surgical mask can block the stench of a mummy's breath.

Her final patient arrives at 4:19 a.m. Their kind is always running late.

Darlene always schedules the newbies last, just in case. The patient waits for her in Exam Room Three.

This room is identical to Exam Room Two, except the chair has metal bands and the dental tray holds no silver instruments. No matter how thoroughly Darlene cleans this room, it still smells vaguely of wet dog. There's always at least one hair clinging to Catherine when she leaves. She closes the door.

The new patient looks about twenty years old, with a Caesar haircut, warm eyes, and predictably stubbly cheeks. He drums his fingers on his lap. His fingernails are dirty, though his hands are well scrubbed. Hairy palms, of course.

"Chris?" she says, and he nods. "This is your first time."

"Yes, it is."

"Did Darlene review the procedure?"

"She did."

Mask. Blue gloves.

"I'll need to strap you in before we begin."

He nods. "I understand."

"I can't give you the anesthetic until you change," she says. "After that, you won't remember a thing." Normally, hygienists can't administer anesthetics, but this isn't a normal practice.

"I've forgotten more than my share of nights," he says. "Especially in the early days. Kinda goes with the territory."

Catherine pulls the metal bands across his shins, thighs, waist, and chest. Even through his clothing, his body heat blushes like a fever. He's not wearing the usual torn clothes and muddy soles. This one has it together. He's been at it for a while. He fits the profile.

"I'll start by reviewing your history." Catherine places his chart on the counter and holds up her pen. "What's your primary birthday?"

"June 2, 1975."

She writes down his answer. "Birthplace?"

"Topeka, Kansas."

"What's your secondary birthday?"

"March 1997." He shakes his head a little, like a flower in the breeze. "Not sure of the day."

"That's fine." She does some mental calculations. "Secondary birthplace?"

"Louisville, Kentucky."

Catherine's heart stumbles over his words. Her blood cells push and shove past each other in her veins like bargain shoppers on Black Friday. Can he smell her excitement?

"You ever visited Lexington?" she says. "I lived there once."

He shrugs, as much as his safety bindings allow. "Yeah. Maybe. I don't know. Those days were a blur. Even now, I can't stay in one place for too long."

"*Even now?*"

"I've gone green. No two-legged meat for me. See, me and the wolf, we have an understanding. It took a long time, but I showed him who the alpha is. I tamed him."

"That's commendable," she says. "And how many times a day do you brush?"

"At least four when the moon is waning. It's like I can't get the taste of it out of my mouth. When the moon's waxing, morning and night. When it's full, it all depends if I can find my toothbrush."

She's doodling now. No point in recording his answers.

"How often do you floss?"

"I don't like having fingers in my mouth."

She holds up a gloved hand. "You've come to the wrong place."

"With the latex, it's fine. It's just . . . I've tasted enough skin."

"You really should floss. Your other self, does it only feed during full moons?"

"Usually. Sometimes a few days before or after."

"What are its dietary preferences?"

He sighs. "Cows, mostly. Dogs or cats, if necessary."

"Just meat, or bones, too?"

The patient winces. "Bones."

"What about before you went green? What did it prefer to eat then?"

"Is this necessary?"

"We need a full medical history, Chris, so we can understand how to treat you. Your kind suffers from some of the worst dental conditions. The biting and chewing, the bad hygiene, and the nature of solenoglyph teeth . . . you're high-risk for many conditions. So tell me, what did your other self prefer to eat?" She's careful to say *what*, and not *who*.

"It seemed to like them young, usually boys."

"I see."

She doesn't bother writing down any more. Instead, she presses the button on the chair. It whirrs in response, and the patient reclines from sitting to almost lying down. He swallows hard. A beard now covers his cheeks.

"You smell like watermelon," he says. "And relief."

"I need to put in the mouth prop before you change." She holds up a metal device fitted with two hinges, a nylon strap, and silicone pads. "It'll keep your—*its*—jaws open during the exam."

"My shoes. Do you mind?"

"Of course." She takes off his loafers and socks, surprised by the smoothness of his bared soles. His toenails are dirty—already sharp. She places his shoes neatly on the floor.

He nods. "Do what you have to do."

She can't meet his gaze. "Okay, open up."

He does.

She works the mouth prop into his mouth, until his jaws are spread open like the belly of a dissected frog. The final metal band holds his forehead in place.

"Whenever you're ready," she says.

His body jerks and twitches. She closes her eyes.

With the prop in place, the patient can't scream. First, she hears his fur sprouting, a scratchy swoosh that sounds like static on the radio. It reminds her of speed-lapse footage of flowers growing, something dynamic that happens every day all around her but too slowly to perceive. Next, the bones. They transform in bursts of splintering snaps, like an oversized bag of popcorn in the microwave. Now comes the leathery squeak of stretching skin. The mouth prop clicks as its hinges adjust to the patient's extending muzzle. The transformation ends with a growl, a rusty motor revved in a dirty garage.

She opens her eyes and gasps.

The beast stares back at her. She knows it well. The brown fur with patterned highlights of black and white. Those yellow hateful eyes. The long sharp teeth.

She locks the door and pulls her silver scaler out of her pocket. The beast's growls deepen, a chainsaw cutting into burnt wood.

"Open up," she whispers.

As she makes her first cut, she remembers her son—not the way he was the night he died, but the way he was as a baby.

He was such a perfect infant with his warm smile and baby powder scent. The milk stains around his lips. The sound of his gentle snoring. The urgent pressure at her breast. She prefers to remember him like that, so pure and genuine. In those few precious months of infant bliss, she found the wholeness that her late husband could never provide. She was complete.

It didn't last.

When her son got older, their harmony fell apart. He grew sullen and willful. He no longer laughed at her jokes. They spent many dinners sitting in painful silence. She grew to despise this spoiled thing that she'd somehow raised. He was no better than his father, possibly worse. In fact, she no longer saw him as a real person but more like one of those mannequins at the mall.

That final night, he rattled off question after question as she led him deeper into the woods. A full moon hovered over the leafless trees.

"This is lame," he said. "Why are we going on a walk so late?"

"Because I have something to show you."

"And it can't wait until morning? I'm missing my shows."

"It has to be now. Tonight."

"Why are you squeezing my hand so tight?"

"Because . . . I love you."

She remembers the feel of his neck—as fragile as a bird— beneath her hands. She kept her eyes closed until he stopped struggling. When it was done, she opened her eyes and gasped. His face no longer looked like a mannequin, more like some cheap Halloween mask. She released him.

He fell to the ground. The loose change in his pocket jingled together a single death note. She took a deep breath.

Her tears spilled downward, hot on her cheek. They felt so genuine. So real. The night was crisper, somehow. The stars above burned brighter. The full moon seemed to shine solely on her. She was whole again. Complete.

Until something growled behind her.

She turned. A horrific beast crouched at the edge of the clearing. Part man, part wolf. Its yellow eyes stared at her, hating her. Judging her. It growled, leapt forward, and knocked her to the ground. The vile thing scooped up the lifeless boy and ran away. Whimpering.

That night, she cried so many tears. She wasn't sad. No, she was angry. It had all felt so real, so crystal clear, until that dirty beast showed up and ruined it.

She never figured out if the monster took her son in a futile attempt to help or if the vile creature simply meant to feed on easy meat.

Honestly, she doesn't care.

She takes her time with the patient, cutting away strips of furry flesh and tearing out all the vital things beneath. He thrashes and whines. His chest rises and falls quickly. Near the end, all the fur falls out, revealing the mutilated man beneath. In this long blissful moment, the emptiness inside her heart fades. She is whole. Complete.

When she's finished with the patient, she bags up the pieces, unlocks the door, and calls for Darlene. The older woman's chair squeaks. Her slow footsteps shuffle down the hall. Darlene opens the door, steps inside over a puddle of blood, and closes the door.

"Can you help me get this room cleaned up?" Catherine says.

"Doctor is going to notice if we keep losing patients."

"He fit the profile."

"So did the last seven." Darlene puts her hands on her hips. "Are you sure? Is this the last time?"

"I think so. I really do"

She chokes back a sob. Her lower lip trembles. Darlene pulls her in and hugs her tight. The old woman smells of baby powder and mints. Her wrinkled hands pat Catherine's head, and that's when the tears come out. She's not sad. She's not even angry, anymore. She's just savoring the moment. It feels so perfect and real.

The crying is such a blessed relief. She savors the tears' clean heat and pure burn. She enjoys it while it lasts.

It never lasts long.

The sun nudges against the horizon when she finally leaves the office. Dead leaves scurry across the asphalt. She clutches her keys tight. The door shuts behind her, and that bell jingles cheerfully behind her.

A Clown and a Dragon Walk Into a Bar

My workday ends with the sound of squealing tires, crackling metal, and choking screams.

The smell of burnt rubber, anti-freeze, and wet copper fills the street. An overgrown Ford pickup had just pulled out of the Shady Pines apartments across the street, colliding head-on with a rusted 60's Cadillac. The driver of the Caddy is trapped behind the wheel, sobbing and picking glass out of his forehead. The other driver – now a tangle of bloody legs and scraped flesh – lies in the street at the end of a blazing comet trail of blood and gore.

Me, I'm standing on the sidewalk in front of Wood Oaks apartments, almost directly across from the accident. In the warm summer breeze, I'm holding seven balloons that tug eagerly at their cords like a litter of leashed puppies. Across the street, in front of Shady Pines, stands a seven-foot-tall dragon, his mouth frozen in a cheerful grin.

Me, I'm Sam the Clown.

Traffic slams to a halt. The dragon and I stare at each other. An eerie peace descends broken only by the sound of fluid spilling out of the wrecked automobiles and the driver sobbing in the Caddy's front seat.

And then the screaming starts.

Somehow, the pickup driver is still alive. She's out in the street wailing like a broken siren. The sound bruises my ears, makes the blood go all bubbly in my veins. I reach in my pocket for my cell, forgetting I'd left it in my locker at the apartment office.

I drop my sign on the curb and walk toward the injured woman – balloons bouncing behind me. The man in the Cadillac stares open-mouthed at me as I shuffle past.

"She came out of nowhere," he says, his deep voice carrying the tone of a fourth grader explaining why he shoved his sister down the stairs. "I didn't see her coming."

I say nothing in response. My clown shoes occasionally snag pavement, causing me to stumble. Sirens blare in the distance.

The woman on the ground says, "Oh God. Oh Jesus. Please help me. Oh God. Oh Jesus. My God."

Oh God. Oh Jesus. That's what Pam used to say during sex. Back when we actually had sex. I push that thought out of my mind as my happy clown shadow falls over the dying woman.

She hears me coming and turns her head. One of her eyes is blood red. When she sees me, she screams. No, wait. She laughs. No, she's definitely screaming. The noise triggers something in the other gawkers nearby. One middle-aged man with a crooked goatee puts himself between me and the woman, and says, "I think you better leave now."

And then I realize how I must look to her, this woman who is clearly dead but doesn't know it yet. Me, a pale-faced, leering clown. Is there anything more terrifying?

I step backward, stumbling over something squishy. The noise of my oversized shoes squashing the poor woman's innards almost makes me heave. I stumble-run back toward the sidewalk, almost tripping over the curb. On hands and knees, I fight back the urge to vomit.

"What the hell?" a familiar voice yells. I turn around to see my boss, Nancy, standing in the apartment office's doorway. She's not wearing shoes. "Clown, go take a break. Come back when the news vans arrive. We couldn't buy this kind of press!"

I shake my head and she disappears back into the office. Soon, a dragon-shaped shadow falls over me.

"Hey," the dragon says. To my surprise, the dragon has a woman's voice. "Want to get a beer?"

*

Last spring, my girlfriend Pam told me she was pregnant. A few weeks later, I quit school, just two quarters shy of a degree in organizational communication – a major that I still don't fully understand. I married Pam and started looking for a job to support us. Of course, no decent place in this economy wanted to hire a guy with 90% of a useless degree. So, I ended up working nights in a warehouse and days at Wood Oaks, an apartment complex on Rolling Hills Road – a stretch of suburban sprawl crowded with apartments, offices, strip malls, and fast food.

Since last June, I've spent five hours a day on the roadside in front of Wood Oaks with a sign reading:

No Deposit!

I wear a painted, round smile, a polka-dotted blue shirt, purple gloves, a round nose, a rainbow wig, and big floppy shoes. The costume is a perfect metaphor for my marriage with Pam. Just like the smile that's painted over my frown, my marriage to Pam is only a loving relationship on the surface. In reality, she's scared I don't love her enough, and I'm angry at her for the clownish hell my life has become.

Every day for the past two months, I've come home covered in grease paint to find her with one or two of her friends, full-time moms who speak their own mom-language. Instead of saying, "She fell down and skinned her knee," they'll say, "She had a whoopsie and got a boo-boo." Instead of saying, "Sam wants to kill himself," they'll say, "Sam isn't wearing his happy face." Which, of course, isn't true. I'm a damn clown. I'm always wearing my happy face.

After her friends leave, we spend most nights watching TV and avoiding each other's gazes. Occasionally, she'll say, "Just tell me you love me, Sam." And I tell her exactly what she needs to hear. Every day, Pam's belly gets a little bit bigger and the lie gets a little bit harder to stomach. No pun intended. Don't get me wrong, I do love Pam. She's a wonderful woman and will be a great mother. But I'm bound to her like one of these magical floating balloons. The thing about magic is, it never lasts. Give it enough time, and the magic dissipates and the balloon shrivels down to a piece of flimsy rubber.

A few weeks back, Shady Pines, the older, cheaper apartment complex across the street from Wood Oaks, hired a walking advertisement of their own: a smiling green dragon with a long foam tail and oversized teeth. His sign read:

No Down Payment!

Right from the beginning, I hated this dragon. Once he showed up, it was like the motorists couldn't even see me. For better or worse, he got almost all of the attention. So, for the past month, the dragon and I have stood across four lanes of busy traffic, enduring the heat, the fumes, passing motorists' obscene gestures, and each other's presence.

Two weeks ago, my boss Nancy gave me a new sign: "We Pay Your Rent." When I asked what that meant, she told me to shut up and get outside. Like most people, she doesn't like clowns. Last week, the dragon got a new sign:

Free Rent!!!

Yes, three exclamation points. Clearly, Shady Pines means business.

*

After tying my balloons to a speed limit sign, I follow the dragon down the sidewalk toward a little bar named 'Doc's' tucked in a strip mall between an electronics shop and a smoothie cafe.

The sweat on my forehead mixes with the white greasepaint, drips into my eyelashes. Already, police cars and ambulances arrive on the scene – men in uniforms yelling, running, and setting up cones to divert traffic down a side street. The woman's cackling screams stop abruptly. I can guess why.

"Hell of a way to get a break," the dragon says, her deep, sultry voice surprisingly not muffled by her costume.

"Yeah."

"I'll take it as I get it, though. I had a late night."

"I know the feeling," I say, newly interested in the dragon. My brain translates *late night* into *I stayed up late drinking because I love to party. Oh, did I mention that I'm into casual sex with clowns?*

We walk side-by-side, not looking at each other. The firefighters on the scene crank up a generator, which drowns out most other noises.

I steal a glance at her costume, surprised at the detailing. Each scale of the dragon's hide looks painted by a caring hand. The dragon's rounded belly – a belly that I swear is bigger than when the summer began – glistens in the sunlight. The eyes are the color of the morning sun. She's a good performer, whoever is inside, wiggling her hips just enough to make her stubby tail sway slightly as she walks. The only flaws in the costume are the cheap rubber hands and plastic teeth, like a mouthful of rounded tombstones.

"I always thought you were a man under that outfit," I tell her as we reach the bar's entrance.

"I thought so."

"Why?"

"Because most men don't spend so much time scratching their balls in front of women."

Shit. I think of all the various rude things I must have done while standing across the street from her. Scratching myself. Picking my nose. Spitting. Ugh. Can she tell that I'm blushing under the makeup? I change the subject.

"I've never seen anything so horrible." I nod toward the accident.

"I have," she says, matter-of-factly. "And beer's just the thing for it."

She swings open the door before I can reach the handle.

"I hope you two brought a punchline in here with you," the bartender says as we, a clown and a dragon, walk into the bar.

"No," the dragon says, "but the priest and rabbi are right behind us."

The bartender laughs and nods, slaps two square napkins on the bar. Aside from the bartender and two old men playing chess, we have Doc's – a cramped little dive that used to be a shoe store – all to ourselves.

I plop onto a barstool and order a beer. I have to keep my clown shoes pointed outward to fit comfortably.

"And for the lizard?" the bartender says.

"I'm a dragon, actually." She slides aside her stool and stands at the bar. "I'll have the same."

I lean toward her. "Say, could you do me a favor?"

"Sure."

"Could you take the top of your costume off? It's kinda distracting."

Before she can answer, the bartender places two bottles in front of us. I place a crumpled five on the bar and motion for him to keep the change.

The dragon looks at me. "I can't. It's a one-piece, and I'm not wearing much underneath."

"Oh." I gulp at my beer, imagine the almost-nude woman inside the dragon. "My name's Sam."

"I'm Carlana."

"So, how'd you get this gig working the road, Carlana?"

"Just lucky, I guess."

I chuckle. "Yeah. Me, too. Beats waiting tables, though."

"I wouldn't know. No one would ever hire me to do that, what with the tail and all."

She wiggles her butt so that her tail shakes back and forth. I laugh and pat her on the shoulder, hoping I'm not being too forward. Her costume is surprisingly firm and leathery. It must be hot as hell in this heat, which means she must be in great shape. And sweaty.

"To working on the road." She holds up her beer.

"To working on the road." I clink my bottle against hers. She leans back and pours beer into the corner of her costume's mouth.

*

Two beers later, Carlana sways lazily on her oversized feet. She's amazing – funny, daring, exciting, and just a bit crude. Such a far cry from what I have waiting for me at home.

"So," I say, "the rope walks back inside and the bartender says, 'Hey, you. Weren't you just in here a few minutes ago?' The rope replies, 'I'm a frayed knot.'"

She laughs so hard that beer shoots out of her flared nostrils.

"Tell me again." I crane my neck to see down her throat. "Exactly how does your suit's drinking system work?"

I'd asked her this earlier, and she'd given some vague explanation of tubing, an internal water bottle, and a pressurized straw – technology developed by Disney for the characters dressed in their theme parks.

"Wow, Sam, you're pretty funny." She ignores my question. "And here I took you for a sad little clown."

"Why's that?"

"Because you always look so pissed off."

"Yeah," I say. "Sam is wearing his angry face."

"Huh?"

"Nothing." I wave a hand dismissively. "It's just... I've had a rough summer. It's not easy being a clown, you know."

She pours a generous gulp of beer into her mouth. "It's not easy being a dragon, either."

"That so?"

She nods, rests her chin on an oversized palm. "We were once a plentiful species, the largest reptile to survive the dinosaur age. But as mankind dominated the globe, we retreated into nature."

I play along. "Makes sense."

"It was not a decision made lightly. After we were driven out of Europe, many advocated an all-out war between dragons and humans. But we dragons are peaceful to a fault. Instead of fighting back, we retreated and let ourselves be hunted almost to extinction."

"It must have been terrible." I pat her scaly arm with mock sympathy. "So, why were you dragon-types hunted? Eat one too many princesses?"

She shakes her head. "We don't eat people. We very rarely breathe fire or terrorize villages. It's because of the gold."

"Gold?"

"We swallow the gold and our digestive systems melt it down to make the shells of our dragon's eggs. It's actually a beautiful process, but try telling that to countries working to maintain a gold standard. They saw us as a threat to their economies, so they slaughtered us."

"I'm so sorry," I say with melodramatic sympathy. "As usual, it all comes down to money."

She nods. "We only survived because of our tears."

"Tears?"

She points to her unblinking eyes. "A dragon's tears bend and fold light, render certain objects almost invisible. It's not so much that you can't see something covered in dragon's tears, as that your eyes see around it. It's a tragic defense mechanism. The more sad and miserable we became, the more we cried and thus were able to conceal ourselves."

I laugh and finish my beer. "Sweetie, you've been wearing that costume too long."

She shrugs and nods. "I can't wait to take it off."

A shiver of anticipation wiggles up my spine. Something magical is happening between us. I take off my purple gloves and toss them on the bar, careful to leave my gold wedding band hidden inside the left glove. "I gotta go to the bathroom."

"I'll order one last round."

*

In the bathroom, I spend an inordinately long time staring at my reflection. The clown staring back at me asks some hard questions.

"Are you really going to cheat on your pregnant wife?"

"What if you make a pass at Carlana and she rejects you? You going to spend the rest of the summer staring across the road at her?"

"What does she look like under that costume?"

I have a distinct moment of clarity, and everything becomes

clear. I love Pam. We have a long road ahead of us, but we just might make it. I'll give myself today as a treat, but moving forward priority one will be providing for Pam and the baby. I'll find some way to do just that.

Back at the bar, Carlana has almost finished her fresh beer. Mine sits next to hers, untouched.

I slide next to her, brush against her dragon thigh. "You're a fast drinker."

She tilts her head, stares at me. "Well, you know. A little beer helps give me the courage to..." She trails off.

"Courage to what?"

"To invite a strange man back to my apartment."

"I'm not so strange."

She taps my clown nose. "Looked in a mirror lately?"

"So, I'm a clown. You're a dragon. Besides, you shouldn't need a beer to invite anyone anywhere. Any man would count himself lucky to be with you. You're funny, smart, and pretty."

"Pretty?"

"Well, yeah. I mean, I imagine you are, under that costume."

"Is... Is the costume pretty?"

I take a drink. "It sure is."

Carlana finishes her beer, slams the bottle onto the counter, and rests a rubbery hand on my shoulder. "Would you like to come back to my place?"

I nod. "Where do you live?"

"Over at Shady Pines." She gestures in entirely the wrong direction.

"Let's go." I chug the rest of my beer and grab my gloves. When I slide my fingers inside, I realize my ring is missing. I leave it.

Outside, firefighters and police officers swarm over the accident scene. The sun sparkles on the broken glass and on Carlana's shiny scales. The firefighters' generator roars, so we don't say much. My balloons still float over at Wood Oaks. When we cross the street near Shady Pines' entrance, the air and asphalt shimmers. Must be the beer.

Carlana leads me inside one of the Shady Pines' rear buildings. Inside the vestibule, she unlocks a door marked "MAINTENANCE" to reveal a wooden staircase.

"The manager lets me live down here practically rent-free."

"That's a sweet deal," I say, pissed at myself for not demanding similar accommodations across the street. Not that Pam would be content to live in the basement of an apartment building.

She motions for me to go down first, and I do.

Into the darkness.

*

Water splashes as my oversized shoes hit the basement floor. A thin sheen of sweat seeps through the greasepaint on my face. I can't orient myself in the muggy darkness, because the sound of dripping water overwhelms my ears.

Carlana brushes past me. I hear something that sounds like a blowtorch sneezing, followed by a blinding explosion of light. Suddenly, Carlana stands in front of me holding an ornate candelabra filled with a dozen lit candles.

She points toward a massive leather recliner sitting in the middle of the room.

"Have a seat, Sam."

I sit and watch while she lights candles hanging from chandeliers, perched on shelves mounted to the walls, and arranged around pools of water. Scattered around the unfinished basement are half-filled bathtubs, sinks, and even one Jacuzzi – all fed by dripping pipes overhead. Carlana steps around jumbled piles of metal – jewelry, candlesticks, coins, spoons, watches, and even a few rectangular bars – covered in greenish rust.

I whistle. "This is something else. Are you some kind of modern artist?"

Carlana walks over to me, slouching so her dragon's head doesn't hit the rafters overhead. "I'm no artist."

I wipe my forehead. "It's hot in here."

"Mind if I undress?" she says.

My heart throbs, both apprehensive and eager. First, she pulls off her gloves, revealing oversized hands covered with the same beautiful scales. Black claws as long as my thumb protrude from each of her six fingers. She tosses aside the gloves and reaches for her face.

I expect her to pull off the top of her costume and reveal underneath a beautiful face and long, blond hair. Instead, she removes the eyes of her costume – two translucent yellow lenses – revealing reptilian yellow eyes with jagged pupils. Next, she pulls a pair of oversized dentures out of her mouth. She places the dentures and contact lenses into a sink and offers me a smile punctuated by razor-sharp teeth.

Oh shit.

I'm about to get out of my seat, but she holds up a hand. *Stay.*

"Carlana, what is this?" I have a distinct moment of clarity, and everything becomes clear. "Are you… All that stuff you said about dragons, it's true, isn't it?"

She sits next to me on the floor, and I'm sure that she's going to bite my face off. Instead, she takes a deep breath and exhales a long puff of smoke through her nostrils. Her brow furrows and her lip pouts outward. I realize then what a great actress she is. All those days by the road and through all those beers at the bar, she kept her face frozen, emotionless.

"But why reveal yourself to me?"

"It's better if I show you." She convulses with a series of hiccups.

I think she's about to puke, but instead she coughs up my wedding ring. Or what's left of it.

"Sorry." She hands it to me. "Couldn't resist."

I stare at the ring, now covered in the same green, flaky rust covering all the piles of junk in the room.

"Why am I here?"

"Because I'm about to give birth, and I can't do it alone."

*

"Carlana, listen," I say, as she lowers herself into the Jacuzzi. "To paraphrase a great movie, I don't know nothing about birthin' no dragons."

Her mass causes water to spill out of the Jacuzzi and soak my shoes. I jump back, cursing. The only thing worse than wearing big clown shoes? Wearing big wet clown shoes.

"You don't need to know anything. Just hold my hand and be encouraging."

She holds out her three-fingered hand. I fight the urge to run, and grasp her hand – cool and dry. She closes her eyes and winces. Her whole body trembles. She arches her back with so much force that I expect the hot tub to snap in two. Then she screams.

Above, someone pounds against the floor and yells, "Shut up down there!"

So this is why she drank so much, to deaden the pain. She grunts again and spreads her legs. Curiosity gets the better of me. I'm not sure if what I see is her vagina or anus, but it stretches wide to reveal the edge of a golden egg. She pushes again and squeezes my hand. Knucklebones grind together. Something snaps inside her hips – like a snake's jaw dislocating to swallow prey – and the orifice spreads still wider.

With one last push, the egg pops out of Carlana and into the water, surrounded by a cloud of blackish green blood. A second later, the egg hits the Jacuzzi's bottom with a metallic clunk – like a boat knocking against a dock. Carlana collapses backward with a splash. A thin vein of smoke rises from her mouth.

"Let me see it," she says, still holding my hand.

I reach my free hand into the water and scoop up the golden egg – easily thirty pounds.

"It's beautiful," she says.

Dragon tears spill out of her eyes, and a shimmer settles over her face and torso. If she wasn't holding my hand right now, I might not notice the seven-foot dragon sitting in the hot tub. It's amazing magic, but not as amazing as the egg.

The golden egg's a perfect sphere the size of a basketball. Never have I seen such a rich luster of gold. I hold it up at my eye level, so that Carlana can see.

And then I bash it over her head.

For the record, I know this is a real shithead thing to do, but with this egg, I can get enough money to start a new life for me, Pam, and the baby.

I wipe the tears from her eyes and smear them over the egg and me. When I reach the stairs, she spits out a string of obscenities punctuated by a jet of fire. The fire grazes my outfit as I bolt upstairs.

Below, she roars. When I open the basement door, a concerned tenant standing in the vestibule jumps backward. He can't see me, but he can sure as hell smell the stink of burnt polyester and singed hair. I brush past him and break for the exit.

Outside, the sunshine tickles my flesh. I run across the Shady Pines complex and into the street.

The generator still roars. Firefighters and police clean up the remains of the accident. I pause at the entrance to Shady Pines where I can easily see over a dozen uniformed public servants. I give them all the middle finger. I grab my balls and stick out my tongue. I pull down my pants and show them my white ass, so pale that it doesn't even need clown make-up.

They don't see a thing.

I notice a familiar shimmer at the Shady Pines entrance. I kneel and examine a sparkling puddle of dragon tears in the street. I look at the accident, and everything becomes clear. Carlana put her tears here to cause an accident, but why? She said that she had a late night... maybe it's because she was out here waiting for an accident that never happened until today. Because she needed someone for the birth. But to what end?

Suddenly, the egg bursts apart in my hands.

Six tiny claws rip through the metal shell, tear it nearly in two. I yell in surprise. The egg's jagged edges cut my hands and I drop it to the asphalt.

When the egg clunks to the ground, a baby dragon jumps out of the broken shell and latches onto my leg. This housecat-sized version of Carlana has the same egg yolk yellow eyes and razor teeth but also has a sharp horn on its snout. I kick futilely with my clown shoe as the little bastard's claws dig into my flesh and scrape my shinbones. With an unmanly scream, I fall to the ground.

None of the policemen or firefighters can see my distress, and the generator mutes my screams. A few policemen look vaguely in my direction before returning to their duties. Grunting and hissing, the baby dragon mounts my chest and slices my cheeks. My red clown nose, now soaked with blood, falls to the ground.

As my vision fails, I see my balloons across the street still tangled and tugging eagerly at their cords. Still desperate to be free.

*

Months pass.

Carlana comes home from work, tosses her *Free Rent* sign into the corner. I'm in the leather recliner, munching on peanuts and sipping a beer. Little Carl leaps into her arms and his forked tongue darts against her cheeks. She pats his back.

I toss a handful of peanut shells onto the floor. "Your son had a whoopsie today. He broke a lamp trying to jump over the Jacuzzi. He lost his egg tooth, too." I proudly hold up the horn that fell off Carl's snout, which Carl used to break out of his egg. At the sound of my voice, Carl leaps onto my chair, nuzzles against my arm. Turns out newborn dragons imprint on their 'parents' as soon as they hatch. Carl wasn't attacking me in the street. He was trying to kiss his daddy.

Carlana takes out her contacts, eyes the horn and then the beer. "You're drinking already?"

I shrug. "Our little man lost his egg tooth. Carl's all excited about the visit he'll get from the egg tooth fairy. I told him he'd get at least five coins. Gold, of course."

Carlana sits on the floor. Her fake teeth are still in, because her fangs creep me out. "Sam, we don't have any more gold coins."

I stand up, flail my arms. "Well excuse me for trying to do something nice for our boy."

She eyes my jiggling belly. "You've put on weight."

"I spend all my time in a cramped, wet basement. What do you expect?"

She reaches back, pulls a beer out of a sink filled with ice. "I'm not in the mood tonight."

I sit back down. "Hard day on the road?"

She nods, holds up her beer.

I clink my bottle against hers. "To working on the road."

"To working on the road," she says, taking a drink.

For a moment, some of that giddy magic inflates between us again. We're two strangers sharing a drink. We crave and care for each other. We're interested. We need each other. The magic is fleeting, but not exhausted. Carl darts and weaves between us, tangles an imaginary cord around us.

I pat Carlana's face. "C'mon, baby. Cry some tears for me. I'll get all invisible and go fetch us some coins. I haven't been out in awhile."

Every week or two, we have an argument and Carlana starts crying. Before storming out, I'll wipe away her tears and smear them over my own face – where eager Carl accidentally carved a permanent smile. Those tears will give me a couple precious hours to walk the streets invisible, steal some money to send to Pam, and sometimes visit her and the baby. I'll stand outside her window and watch her nurse our baby. It's a girl. I don't know her name.

Carlana frowns. "I sometimes wonder if you won't come back."

I point at my scarred cheeks. "With a smile like this, I'm not eager to be seen by anyone. I don't have anywhere else to go. And besides that, I'm not looking." Carl scampers across the room, knocks over my television. I look at Carlana and sigh. "You and Carl are my life now, Car."

A tear blossoms in her eyes. "That's sweet, Sam."

"Just tell me you love me."

She offers me her plastic smile, wipes a tear from her eye, and tells me what I need to hear.

GAG

Malcolm Sever watches his lover Mandy, wearing only a bathrobe, chase an old man through a hardware store's front window. Caked in blood, she's barely recognizable. She makes that horrid noise that all of the Retches make – like a cat choking on a hairball.

The old man screams for help – an instinct from a lost world. Months ago, his plea would have summoned a whole entourage: police officers, ambulances, and news vans. But that was before the G.A.G.

Broken glass grinds under Mandy's bare feet, like a snowman gritting its teeth. Malcolm's cell phone vibrates yet again. He answers, though cell towers haven't operated for months. Only Shades use the phones now.

"Yeah?" he says.

It's Mandy, talking all lowercase and no punctuation: "...ever really love you i mean you are a nerd i once hit a cat with a belt buckle the sky tastes like stale cotton candy i faked an orgasm because your goatee was tickling..."

"Mandy," he says over her, "your body just ran into a hardware store. I'm going in after you. I'll save you. Just like I promised, hon."

"...drunk and there were at least two of them that i remember and the next morning i didnt even care i once jerked off a cocker spaniel hispanics scare me i hated the godfather part two you dont mean anything to me ive only ever used you for..."

"Today I'm going to save the world," he says. What's left of it.

*

Nine months ago.

Malcolm heard about G.A.G. for the first time while smoking on the roof of the Village Tower apartment building. He was with Paul, the crackpot from down the hall. Paul rolled his own smokes, crooked things that stuck to Malcolm's lip and made it bleed.

"You heard about the G.A.G. yet?" asked Paul, blowing smoke into the cold morning air.

"What gag?" asked Malcolm.

Below, Mandy crossed the street. They watched as she staggered into the Village's front door. Another late night.

Paul shook his head. "It's an acronym. Stands for *Ghosts And Ghouls*."

Malcolm rolled his eyes. "Another government conspiracy?"

"Maybe." Paul grunted and flicked his cigarette over the edge of the building. Even that slight movement caused his thick arm muscles to flex dramatically. "The Internet said when someone gets the G.A.G., their mind is torn from the body. They're split in two: a ghost and a mindless body, like a zombie. The radio said last week in Arkansas, an infected priest's ghost sent emails to his congregation – exposing all manner of perversion and corruption – while his body raised hell in a nursing home."

Freed from the body, these Shades sought out loved ones, hated ones, or even just their barber. By interfacing with audio technology, the Shades spoke the harshest truths, every secret once crammed inside their skulls.

"Bullshit."

"Maybe so." Paul shrugged. "But you should consider stocking up on canned food and ammo."

That was Paul's solution to everything.

"I don't have a gun, Paul."

"You want one?"

Malcolm waved a hand dismissively. "What presumably causes G.A.G.?"

"I hear the CIA was testing a new interrogation technique. Other possibilities are the latest flu vaccine, a strain of genetically modified poultry, or a smart phone app."

"Paul, I'm a brain man." That's how Malcolm always referred to his area of scientific inquiry. "And I have to tell you that this is one of your more interesting fringe conspiracies." Malcolm punched Paul's generous biceps. "Did you know that a pound of human brain burns twenty times the calories as a pound of human muscle?"

"Huh."

"It's true. Your brain makes up two percent of your body weight but uses about twenty percent of your body's total energy."

Below, someone yelled. Malcolm glanced down in time to see an old lady sprinting after a teenager. The granny, easily in her sixties, was gaining on the teen.

"So, tell me, Paul, what would a body do with all that extra energy if the brain no longer needs it?"

*

Mandy moshes through the aisles amidst a crowd of paint cans, shovels, oscillating fans, and power tools. The last scraps of sunlight bellycrawl under the hardware store's awning.

While Shades are concerned with secret obsessions, their mindless bodies – known as Retches – just want to bite and screw, spreading the disease. Retches prefer human prey, though they settle for animals or even leather furniture as a last resort.

On the security mirrors, Malcolm sees the old man hiding behind a spackle display. He's clutching a mallet and panting like a dog, but Mandy's too stupid to hear. Her frenzied dance approaches the old man with the mallet.

Near the cash register, Malcolm grabs a cheap flashlight from the check-out display. With shaking hands, he shines a jittery beam of light on the old man.

Blindly, the old man hurls the mallet past Malcolm's head.

Mandy knocks the geezer onto a mound of spackle buckets. As she bites his face and dry humps his abdomen, a look of recognition flashes over the old man's surprised face.

With one breast dangling from under Malcolm's fuzzy blue robe, Mandy spits out a lump of flesh, takes another bite. She's not eating, just biting.

Malcolm's cell vibrates in his pocket. He ignores it, retrieves the mallet.

As he stalks down an aisle, Mandy's voice bursts over the store intercom, the sound cranked to eleven: "...glad that he committed suicide it was like winning the lottery i spit in your coffee i stole mr. pacernick's grade sheet and no one ever knew one time i touched my brother's..."

Damn it. Must hurry now. A noise like that could attract the Gaggle.

Ahead, the old man's whole body flops like a fish out of water and goes still. An icy breeze whistles over Malcolm's skin, the old man's soul swirling upward. His body spasms to life, then he and

Mandy lunge at each other in a lustful tangle.

If Malcolm let them go at it, they'd ravage each other for hours, biting and kissing and slobbering and grinding.

Sure, Malcolm's jealous.

Now it's the old man's voice over the intercom. "...bEAT hER a tIME oR tWO bUT sHE hAD iT cOMING i pOISONED a lITTER oF pUPPIES bECAUSE i hATED tHE wHINING i cANT sTAND wHINING iM aFRAID oF nEED i sTOLE fROM tHE..."

Dammit. Malcolm hates togglecase. It gives him a headache.

Malcolm pulls out the hypodermic he borrowed from Paul's medical kit. The old man is on top of Mandy now, hips pounding. Malcolm injects Mandy's ankle with a sedative. She goes limp, but the old man doesn't notice. Malcolm swings the mallet and bashes his skull.

Almost instantly the Shade's voice fizzles on the intercom. "...cHURCH i fUCKED mISSUS mONROE... iN hER oWN lIVING... rOOM aND wIPED mYSELF oFF oN hER cURTAINS aND nEVER... cALLED hER bY... hER fIRST..."

Malcolm fastens zip-ties around Mandy's wrists. Something clicks insider her throat with every ragged exhalation. He sits her up, cradles her beautiful face. Her arched eyebrows. Her tangled red hair. Her thin lips.

"I'm going to save you," he says. "I'm going to save the world."

Mandy's head jerks reflexively to one side, biting a gumdrop-sized lump of flesh from Malcolm's hand. Almost instantly, Malcolm's blood feels like used motor oil.

Soon, he'll hack up his soul.

*

Seven months ago.

Teens danced to the Retched Rumble. G.A.G. t-shirts were banned from public schools. The wealthy paid top dollar to have sex with Retches, so long as they were properly masked. The world had G.A.G. fever.

The hottest reality show on t.v., *G.A.G. My Wife, Please*, was about a man coping with his G.A.G.-infected wife. Malcolm watched the show while helping Paul can two hundred pounds of tomatoes.

On the screen, the husband sat next to his wife's cage. She thrashed and gyrated against the bars, while her Shade rambled on a monitor. "...tHE tOILET sEAT dOWN yOU dONT kNOW hOW tO eAT mY – bleep – iVE hAD bETTER – bleep – fROM sTRAY cATS i hATE yOUR mOTHERS cHICKEN..."

"Okay, brain man," Paul said. "Tell me how humans can be so smart yet so dumb."

Malcolm shrugged. "Our brains are one-point-nine percent of our bodies, compared to the lion – only one percent. Since our ancestor *Homo genus* emerged 2 million years ago, the human brain has doubled in size."

"Wouldn't know it to watch this shit."

"Yes, but why'd we evolve so much extra brain weight?"

*

Malcolm drags Mandy outside. With his hands under her arms, he feels the spastic pulse common to all Retches.

No rhythm.

No pattern.

No rhyme.

Already, that jangly offbeat song invades Malcolm's chest. His heart burps and clenches. His vision is flattening out, the world losing all depth. His skull is a fragile eggshell. Great. Now he's recycling old Jim Morrison metaphors.

This is the end. His only friend.

No it isn't.

The sky is an upset belly with indigestion and heartburn. On the horizon, the sun dissolves like an effervescent tablet, offering no real relief.

Malcolm stumbles against the van, hoisting Mandy through the rear doors. He falls inside and slams the doors shut. Strapping her into the backseat, he fumbles the key into the ignition and latches his seatbelt. The engine groans awake, and Mandy's voice tumbles over the radio on a bed of static.

"...was my father but he never suspected i used to cut myself when that didnt work i cut other people not with blades but words i think doves have no souls i whispered dirty words all through the pledge of..."

The van lurches down the street. Malcolm's throat clicks. His heart trembles.

He's not going to make it.

*

Five months ago.

G.A.G. mutated. Or maybe not. Maybe the line between humanity and technology dissolved. Over the course of a week, G.A.G. spread through email attachments, smart phones, and viral marketing. The government pulled the plug on the Internet, but it was too late. Cities were overrun. Highways were clogged. G.A.G. was everywhere, and no one was ready for it.

No one except Paul.

He rallied the Village tenants together and turned the building into a fortress complete with compost toilets and solar power.

Malcolm had never known many of his fellow Village tenants, had only ever cared to know one –Mandy. For years, he felt a familiar ping in his heart whenever he passed her in the halls. Pre-G.A.G., she wouldn't give Malcolm the time of day. After G.A.G., she visited regularly to watch movies and listen to music on his home entertainment system.

One afternoon, Malcolm sat on his couch, watching Mandy do sloppy yoga wearing only a pair of short-shorts and an "I G.A.G. FOR THE TRUTH" t-shirt. No bra.

"You think we're okay here?" Mandy said.

Malcolm shrugged. "Paul's kept us all safe so far."

Outside, the street was all screaming, gagging, and static-filled ranting. Malcolm never thought he'd miss the sound of traffic, car alarms, and thumping bass.

Mandy rose into the cobra position, her pelvis grinding against the floor and her chest arching upward.

"Give me a drag," she said.

Malcolm held one of his last cigarettes to her lips. She took a drag, exhaled. Malcolm glanced down her shirt.

"I'd kill for some good drugs," she said. "Can't you synthesize something, science boy?"

"No drugs. I worked in porn tech."

She looked him in the eye. "That so?"

"I was a security consultant. Developed fixes for viruses. Remember last year, when people kept falling in love with virtual partners?"

"Yeah."

"I developed the love patch to fix that." Malcolm held up a flashdrive. "I've got a copy of the love virus right here."

Mandy laughed. "The love patch. That's great." She lowered

her chest to the ground, hands folded under her chin. "Could have used the love patch when I was little and Mom left my dad. She fell in love with some dick named Tim, ran off on us." She stared at the window. "I hope he's okay."

"Who? Tim?"

"No, dumbass. My dad." She rolls up her sleeve, revealing her dad's portrait tattooed on her shoulder. "He lives right near here, by that playground on Fourth Street. We used to play on the seesaw there all the time. I haven't talked to him in years. He was the only thing that ever kept me grounded."

Malcolm interrupted, "When you're in love, the brain's ventral tegmental is overactive. It produces dopamine, providing pleasure and motivation. It's not unlike cocaine."

Mandy eyed the flashdrive, licked her lips. "You're saying, when you're in love, you're high?"

Malcolm nodded. "There are few limits to what a love-drunk heart would do."

*

A block later, Malcolm's heart becomes a ball of yarn ravaged by kittens. Sweat soaks his shirt. The G.A.G. – even from its entry at the extremities – spreads quickly through his body. He pats the patch stuck behind his ear to make sure it hasn't come loose.

He's still blocks away from the Village when convulsions wrack his chest. His heartbeat tugs like a frantic fish hooked on a line.

He grunts.

The van swerves onto the sidewalk. Malcolm fights the steering wheel. The van plows into the corner of a credit union. The impact throws Malcolm through the windshield and into a concrete wall. He lands in a heap.

That jangly heartbeat is gone.

*

Three months ago.

Malcolm and Mandy lay in bed, the sheets littered with various sex programs and pornware. Malcolm asked a stupid question.

"Are you fucking serious?" Mandy said. "We're living in the post-apocalypse, and you're asking me what's wrong?"

But for Malcolm, it hadn't been a stupid question. For Malcolm, life had only gotten better since the G.A.G.

"I just want everything back to normal," she said. "That's all I want."

"Then that's what I'll do. I'll make everything better."

She took off her pleasure-goggles and laughed. "Malcolm, you're a porn tech." She lovingly patted the stimulator strapped to her thigh. "A really good porn tech, but really? What are you going to do?"

He pulled off his prototype love-glove and holstered his disinhibitor gun. "Hon, I had Fortune 500 companies knocking on my door straight out of college. I just didn't want to deal with the..."

She arched her eyebrow and rubbed his crotch with her foot. "The pressure?"

"The bullshit. I've got a knack for figuring things out."

She rolled her eyes. "Delusional much?"

"If I say I can do this, I can." He held up a transdermal patch. "This is a patch I developed for PornMaker 3.4. Because of the software's heightened connectivity, we needed a way to keep the customers from either contaminating the host software or picking up an STD from the host."

"STD?"

Malcolm nodded. "Simulation Technology Disease. I can modify the patch to keep the wearer's consciousness intact once the body gets G.A.G. The wearer would be a Shade, but a rational one."

Mandy rolled her eyes. "Uh-huh."

"If I could wear the patch and get infected with G.A.G., I could study it from outside the body. It's like fixing a car." Malcolm slid his hand under Mandy's shirt. "To diagnose the problem, you have to get out from behind the wheel. Under the hood."

"Is it really that simple?"

Malcolm nodded. "No. Not at all. Nothing about the brain is simple. Did you know that more electrical impulses are generated in one day by a single human brain than by all the telephones in the world?"

"Including texts?" she said.

*

Malcolm has no heartbeat. He lies on dirty cement waiting for death's fabled white light. He feels no pain, so must be either paralyzed or dead.

But wait. He was wearing his seatbelt, so how could he have been thrown from the van? He opens his eyes and turns his head, expecting to hear vertebrae cracking like celery. The van's windshield is mostly intact. It wasn't his body that was thrown from the van. It was his Shade.

He must have gagged-out when the van made impact. Patch 2.0 worked. He's rational. He shakes his head, the motion sending comet trails across his vision. He looks at his ghostly hands, and it's like staring cross-eyed – seeing each eye's image crossed over the other, neither image really substantial. He's seeing past and future with no present.

He staggers toward the van, his steps unsteady not from trauma but from the energy and thought and feeling swirling all around him.

Mandy's Shade crawls on all fours over and under the wreckage, muttering to herself. "...put the cards back in the deck but fuck it right blind children have more money than they know what to..."

Even without her body, she's beautiful.

Malcolm sees the open driver's door and freezes. The front seat is empty, the tattered seatbelt dangling. His body somehow unlatched the belt and escaped. Damn it. Without his body, he's just a lost ghost. Can this day get any worse?

From blocks away, he hears the hacking and lurching. A flesh amoeba with thousands of feet, hands, and eyes – half as many mouths.

The Gaggle.

*

One month ago.

The Gaggle passed by the Village – a mob of hundreds, maybe thousands, of infected Retches. A storm cloud of heaving flesh acting under a singular hive mind. Bite. Fuck. Grow.

A flock. A murder. A school.

The Gaggle.

Down the street, a flashlight blinked repeatedly from a Mexican restaurant's roof. A band of survivors had holed up there for weeks. The Gaggle hit the restaurant like a mammalian tsunami. The Retches climbed one upon the other, stretching up the building. Inside, women and children screamed.

"Mandy says you're working on a cure," Paul said.

"I'm trying."

As if on cue, Mandy walked onto the roof, stood between

Malcolm and Paul. "You got your night goggles, Paul?"

He handed them to her. Malcolm watched to see if their hands touched.

"They're so creepy," Mandy said, training the goggles on the Gaggle. She shivered.

He stroked her thigh. "I don't think it's a 'they' anymore. It's an 'it.'"

"What makes it happen?" she said.

Malcolm shrugged. "Ever watch a flock of birds? They land, fly, and change course as one. To watch it, you'd think the birds' brains were somehow networked. But really it's just emergent behavior. The group moves based on decisions of individual birds, following simple rules responding to neighboring birds. It all happens in a quick chain reaction."

He stared at the edge of the Gaggle. A shirtless teenager with a broken nose. Someone's grandmother, topless and shriveled. A heavily-tattooed Asian wearing snow boots. What did they all have in common? Each other.

Paul snorted. "Way to take the romance out of migration."

Mandy nodded. "To hear you talk sometimes, you'd think the soul was nothing more than an email attachment."

"Nah, souls are huge," Malcolm said. "They'd crash all the servers in heaven."

She elbowed him. "Shut up."

He ignored her. "The slowest speed that information travels between neurons is about 260 mph. Our brains can make 20 million billion calculations per second. How fast could brains compute if they were networked? Can you imagine the speed?"

*

Malcolm's Shade sprints through the street.

No, literally. He trips and phases through the street into a sewer tunnel below. It takes him way too long to climb back to street level. By that point, the Gaggle is closing in. If the Gaggle finds the van, it'll absorb Mandy. He'll lose her forever.

He takes a deep breath, realizes that he has no lungs, and goes through the motion of exhaling anyway. Retches and their Shades are never far apart, so his body should be nearby. Like a shadow turned inside out, he sees a faded line leading around the corner – his connection to his retched body.

Malcolm sprints after the line and finds his body humping away on the busted remains of someone's Harley Davidson. The Gaggle comes into sight, a couple blocks away.

Malcolm's body dismounts the bike and stumbles toward the Gaggle.

Shit.

Malcolm catches up to his body halfway down the street and tries throwing himself into his own head. It doesn't work. Frantic, he remembers a diagram of the body's chakras and tries slamming his consciousness into every one of these holes. No good.

He recalls Mandy's words from last month. File attachments. Of course. His consciousness is too big. It has to be compressed and encrypted. Parsed. He jumps piggyback onto his body and begins shoving bits of himself inside. His favorite color, pea green. The taste of stale beer. His first day of kindergarten. The smell of his father's shoes.

He shoves until there's nothing left.

*

Earlier this afternoon.

Malcolm left his lab early, wearing a triumphant grin. Patch 2.0 was ready for field-testing. Malcolm rubbed the patch against his neck. But where the hell was Mandy? Malcolm checked her apartment and the stairwell, where he found Paul wearing only a t-shirt and a pair of jeans. Unusual to see him unarmed.

"Paul? You seen Mandy?"

He stared at the floor. "Haven't seen anyone all afternoon."

Downstairs, someone screamed and hacked. Wood splintered and glass shattered.

They ran down the stairs, only to find the lobby trashed. A dead Retch lay sprawled on the dusty tile, still twitching. Outside, Mandy ran down the street, wearing Malcolm's bathrobe. Why was she down here? Wearing only a bathrobe?

Malcolm held out his hand. "Give me the van key, Paul."

Paul shook his head. "You'll never find her. I can't risk losing the van."

"Paul, I'm a brain man. There are 100,000 miles of blood vessels in the brain. And one hundred billion neurons. If I can navigate that mess, you think I can't find Mandy?"

*

Malcolm tastes grit and tire tread. He's face-down in the street. He did it. He actually parsed his soul back into his body. His smile soon fades at the sound of several thousand feet plodding against asphalt. The Gaggle's coming this way.

Malcolm sprints back to the van. The Gaggle thunders behind him, each of its synchronized steps shaking the ground. Or maybe the Earth's just frightened.

At the van, Mandy's soul mutters, "...to the police because i hated the sound of her voice i took the last cookie and..."

"Hang on, hon," Malcolm says, sliding into the driver's seat. Behind him, Mandy's body thrashes and hacks.

The keys jingle in the ignition. Malcolm turns the key, but the engine only clicks lamely. Malcolm slams his head against the steering wheel. He has to get Mandy away from—

A wave of appendages pounds and stomps the van, nearly knocking it over. The Gaggle eclipses any light from the sky above.

"I just had a really bad idea, Mandy," Malcolm says. He steps into the rear of the van, grabs her by the hair, and holds his forearm to her mouth. "Bite me, hon."

Moments later, Malcolm's Shade flows out of the van. The Gaggle's Shades dance in the sky, sparkling flames rising from the coals of flesh. Will this work?

It has to.

Malcolm tears himself apart, parsing his soul into thousands of packets and hurling each packet into the hollow minds below. A fat black man tastes Malcolm's grandmother's blueberry pie for the first time. A tattooed divorcee writes shitty poetry in Malcolm's high school journal. A one-eared attorney loses his virginity on Malcolm's parents' bed.

And so it goes.

Suddenly, the Gaggle's hacking rhythm, the noise that's haunted the city for weeks, goes silent. It's an eerie silence, punctuated by thousands of Retches simultaneously taking in an in-breath.

Malcolm is the Gaggle. His thoughts are amplified by thousands. His feelings stream fast and rich. Everything's déjà vu. For a long while, the Gaggle stands mute, swallowing periphery vision to the hundredth power.

His thoughts, once clouds, rain freely. No, they pour. In great bursts, his ideas puddle and flood his networked consciousness. Lightning flashes all strobe. Unfiltered thoughts overflow his thousand skulls.

Quickly, the revelation comes.

Back at the lab, he has a disinhibitor gun, a cheap plastic toy used to unwind anxious lovers. With a few simple tweaks, he can modify the gun into a cure. One shot, and the Retch's soul will return to its body.

Malcolm's going to save the world.

Not a particularly coordinated man even when operating only one body, it takes Malcolm Gaggle a long while to push the van back to the Village. Bodies crash to the ground. He steps with thousands of feet. His pulse echoes in as many hearts.

Above, the Gaggle's orphaned souls expand – dry sponges soaked in water – and glow like fireflies. With their bodies now occupied, the souls are heading for that fabled light. If Malcolm doesn't leave the Gaggle soon, its souls will be lost forever.

At the Village, Malcolm Gaggle shoves the van backwards through the front doors, effectively blocking the entrance.

Malcolm Gaggle kneels.

He ejects.

*

Earlier this evening.

Malcolm drove through the streets, thinking of the places Mandy talked about. Clubs. Dive bars. Music shops. Where could she be?

Of course. He turned west, onto Fourth Street. The playground. Sure enough, Mandy was there, flopping up and down on a seesaw covered in blood. He needed a distraction. Nearby, an old man watched from behind one of the school's boarded-up windows. Malcolm inhaled deeply and waved at the man. The man smiled and waved back.

Malcolm's phone vibrated. It was Mandy.

"...starved my goldfish al pacino is overrated i secretly envy religious people i once pissed on a sleeping..."

Malcolm opened the passenger door. The old man limped toward the van. His grey hair was the color of rainy sky. Even from here, Malcolm recognized the face that countless times had stared back from Mandy's shoulder.

Mandy's father.
Ten steps away.
Nine.
Eight.

That's when Malcolm hit the horn and closed the door. The old man's eyes went wide. Mandy leapt off the seesaw and sprinted across the playground. She sure as hell wasn't running away from daddy anymore.

Malcolm spoke into the phone, ignoring Mandy's confessional gibberish. "Mandy, each of our hundred billion neurons makes contact with thousands of other neurons via synapses. Our brains make about a million of new connections per second, those connections' strength and pattern always changing. With all that in mind, how can two people's love be anything but temporary?"

*

Malcolm's Shade dives through the van's roof. The Gaggle flails over the van and against the Village. Meanwhile, Mandy thrashes and hacks. He can't take her upstairs like this, so he parses himself into her body as well as his own.

Moving as one, he runs on four legs up the Village's staircase. Yes, he takes a moment to cop a feel with Mandy's own hands. When Malcolm enters his loft, Mandy's soul – already shimmering toward the light – rambles through his speakers, "...her we were only friends the bitch bought it i undertipped because she was prettier than..."

Malcolm sits at his desk, funneling his theories and concepts through his fingertips. Working with two bodies, he quickly builds the soul-inhabitor gun.

He tunes out the noise of the Gaggle storming the building, breaking windows, tearing down walls. He blocks everything but Mandy's voice.

Because it isn't there.

While Malcolm puts the finishing touches on his soul-inhabitor, he sends Mandy's body into the hallway to find her Shade. It takes concentration, being two places at once. But he needs Mandy's Shade here with her body, for a first test.

Malcolm-Mandy finds her Shade on the fire escape. There, Paul throws bricks down at the Gaggle below – splattering chunks of Retch skull all over the sidewalk.

Mandy's voice comes from his walkie talkie. "...love you i need you we are meant for each..."

Paul turns around and sees Mandy. He rears back to throw a brick at her. His vision darts from the walkie talkie to Mandy's body.

"other i think of you when i'm fucking malcolm i just want..."

Paul lunges for Mandy and kisses her. He tastes like tic-tacs and gun powder.

Son of a bitch. That's why Mandy left the loft in her bathrobe – to meet Paul for a secret rendezvous. While Paul's kissing Malcolm-Mandy, Malcolm-Malcolm grabs the soul-inhabitor and strides down the hall.

Malcolm-Mandy pushes Paul away just as Malcolm arrives. Seeing Malcolm, Paul chucks the walkie talkie – with Mandy still chattering – down at the Gaggle.

Malcolm-Malcolm aims the soul-inhabitor at the Gaggle, ready to save the world.

But wait...

He can finally see how selfish he's been.

"Is that loaded?" Paul says.

"No, Paul. It's junk," Malcolm-Malcolm and Malcolm-Mandy say simultaneously.

Paul eyes them both warily. Malcolm laughs, throws the soul-inhabitor down into the Gaggle. It shatters in pieces.

"Paul," he says. "You taste like gunpowder."

Without another word, he and Mandy return to his loft. He ejects from Mandy, and she lunges at him. His Shade floats upward as he and Mandy buck and wiggle together – a beast with two heads, four arms, and four legs.

Malcolm parses himself once again into the Gaggle's hungry flesh. Now free of his body, his thoughts are free to rain.

Free to reign.

He's been so selfish. So stupid. The world doesn't need saved.

It needs rebooted.

Knowing the apartment's defenses, he easily overtakes the Village and converts Paul and everyone inside – except the Retch bodies of himself and Mandy. They deserve each other.

Meanwhile, Malcolm has a world to rebuild.

One body at a time.

In unison, thousands of voices speak with raspy voices:

"Welcome to Malcolm Village."

*

One week later.

He systematically takes over the whole city until he spans hundreds of thousands of bodies. Millions of fingers all at his will. Trillions of synapses flutter at his command.

"Welcome to Malcolm City."

*

One month later.

"Welcome to Malcolm Country."

*

Nine weeks later.

"I did it. I saved the world... Malcolm World."

Bump

A stranger is coming to kill Patricia, and all she can think about is vacuuming her apartment.

She runs the vacuum across the carpet. Its vague roar consumes Patricia, gives her something to focus on besides her body. Besides Cal.

Cal knew a lot about creating stories. He once told her that every good story starts with a moment that changes everything – a dividing line between then and now. For Patricia, that moment was a year ago.

Then, she vacuumed monthly. Now, at least once a day. Then, she started her day with a cup of coffee. Now, she never drinks caffeine. Then, she slept seven hours straight through the night. Now, she's lucky to sleep two straight hours. Then, she brushed her teeth morning and night. Now, she brushes almost hourly. It's the only way to get the taste of Cal out of her mouth.

Knock. Knock. Knock.

Barely hearing the knock at the door, she pulls the plug out of the wall without turning the vacuum off. Almost instantly, something foreign rattles inside her belly, tickling her insides. She opens the door, expecting a priest in a feather headdress? Perhaps a robed stranger carrying a wooden stick?

Nope. Instead, she's greeted with a warm smile by a slightly stooped guy with oversized glasses. He looks like a hotel concierge.

"I'm Carter." He picks up an oversized briefcase from the welcome mat. She ushers him inside, and he heaves his briefcase onto the couch. "Nice place. Very tidy."

"I clean a lot."

He chuckles. "So do I." He opens the case, revealing an assortment of vials, gleaming tools, and dirty leather bags. "So, where do you want to die?"

Patricia's heart stumbles. The skin over her right hip swarms as if infested with bees. She fights the urge scratch herself raw.

She shrugs. "Where would you recommend?"

"Wherever you'll be most comfortable."

*

"You're making me uncomfortable," she told Cal. "Slow down."

This was more than a year ago. They were coming from a friend's party. Cal's car sped down the country road, such that the trees along the road seemed to spin haphazardly.

"If you have something to say, just say it, Cal. But don't drive like a jerk. I don't appreciate it."

"You don't—" He flailed his arms. "You're such a child when you drink."

"I'm the child? You insisted on being the designated driver. I offered to drive. Don't get mad because I had a good time."

While she drank merlot wine at the party, Cal had sipped on coffee the entire time – black and loaded with sugar. Now, he was all jittery. He'd probably be up all night. Talking to her. Touching at her.

"You don't even know what you did wrong, do you?"

"Did wrong? So, you're judging me now?"

Ahead, a golden retriever crossed the road. She shouted for Cal to stop, and he swerved off the road. The car rolled and crunched into the earth. By the time the ambulance arrived, he was dead and she was unconscious.

She spent three days in the hospital. Two days after going home, she discovered the bump.

*

"So, you get rid of things that go bump in the night?" asks Patricia. "How'd you get into this business?"

Carter stands over her, pouring little mounds of red powder on the bed. "I used to be a chef," is all he says, as if that explains everything.

Patricia is lying down, covered only by a towel. An invisible hand taps its fingers against her spinal cord. She knows this motion. Cal used to tap his fingers on the kitchen table like this while Patricia was in the middle of one of her long, rambling stories.

"I never dreamed I'd do this for a living," adds Carter.

"Well, I never thought I'd do this for a dying."

Carter chuckles. "Clients aren't usually funny. Thanks."

"No, thank you. I'm unraveling here. I just want to be at peace. I can't go on like this."

Nodding sympathetically, Carter wipes two silver rods with what smells like a spicy Asian dipping sauce. After spraying a blue mist into the air, he waves the rods around, studies the air, then nods, apparently satisfied.

"It's a sunny Wednesday afternoon," says Patricia. "Doesn't really seem to fit, does it?"

"Would you prefer I come back on a full moon night? Perhaps a Saturday with thunderstorms?"

Patricia frowns. "This'll do. Nothing real is ever like it would be in a story. That's what I tried telling Cal so many times. But for him, we were a fairy tale. Happy ever after."

Carter examines a profile sheet that they'd completed earlier, detailing her age, weight, height, blood pressure, blood type, and so on. He'd examined her thoroughly, tapping each of her teeth with an iron rod, measuring the circumference of her ears, counting the hazel flecks in her irises, and making several illegible notes about her navel. Now, he adds pinches of powder to a glass of what looks like dirty water. Patricia sniffs the drink, expecting it to stink of death. Instead, she smells spiced flowers and moist dirt.

"Chamomile makes it more palatable," he says. "Drink every last drop."

She takes it all down, and lies back on the bed. The liquid warms her belly like a ray of sunshine. Gradually, the warmth fades, and she feels absolutely normal.

"I don't think it's working," she says.

"It's working." Carter stares at his notebook, then stares at the ceiling as if doing math in his head. "This is going to hurt quite a bit."

*

"Does it hurt?" asked her sister Payton, running her fingers over the bump on Patricia's hip.

Patricia shook her head. "Sometimes it aches." Patricia pulled up her skirt, revealing her inner thigh. "Watch my thigh while you press on the bump."

As Payton pressed down on the bump on Patricia's hip, an identical bump appeared on Patricia's inner thigh.

"He used to hold me there at night, Paypal."

"What the hell's going on? You missed Christmas. You haven't returned my messages. And you look like hell."

Patricia smiles, points at her gleaming teeth. "Yeah, but my teeth have never looked better."

"Pats, c'mon."

Patricia put her hand over her sister's, holding it against the hip bump. "Do you feel the bump's pulse? It's not mine. Sometimes it's faster. Usually slower. Sometimes it's the beat of songs we used to dance to."

Payton pulled her hand away. "Can't you just have it removed?"

"It hides from doctors. I've tried cutting it out myself."

Patricia pulled up her shirt, revealing the ugly scar on her breast. "It just comes back somewhere else. It's Cal. He's haunting me. When I try to sleep, he tickles my flesh, knocks on my bones. I feel his hands on my breasts. In my breasts."

"In your breasts?"

Patricia nods. "He once told me that if he had my body, he'd never go out. He'd just touch himself all day. He would go on and on about how much he loved me, but I swear he just loved my body."

"Pats, if you have a ghost, just leave. Move in with me."

"He's not haunting this apartment." She grabbed Payton to make sure this next part sank in. "He's haunting my body. He's inside me."

Payton nodded. "We'll find someone who can help."

"Who?"

*

"Carter!" Patricia calls out, as a wave of agony rolls over her insides. A murder of crows flaps and claws in her stomach. A clowder of cats slashes and tangles her veins.

Meanwhile, Carter waves his silver wands over the bed, as if prodding at an invisible octopus. Patricia tries to scream, but her lungs are frozen. Her vision crackles, fades. She hears nothing but her own heartbeat. And Cal's.

And then suddenly the pain is gone.

She sits up, a sensation like Velcro tearing apart. Sitting next to her on the bed is Cal, staring dumbly at her. They're both naked, except their finer features are blurred – as if they were made of wax and had melted in the sun.

Oh my, the sun.

In the distance is a startlingly bright light –as bright as the sun but as soothing as the moon. Its light passes through everything. Bits of Cal and Patricia flake away, spilling toward the light. She's vaguely aware of Carter using his wands to wrangle these bits of them floating away.

"Did you miss me?" asks Cal.

"When did I have the opportunity to miss you? You were kissing the inside of my throat at your own funeral, Cal. Why are you haunting me? Was it the party – our argument after? Tell me what I did wrong, Cal."

He shakes his head. "I just want to be close to you. I'm lonely."

Patricia points at the light. "So go there! Can't you hear all those voices? Don't you feel how peaceful it is? It's calm. Go there." As she says these words, she can't take her eyes off the light. It's so inviting. True peace. "The fairy tale's over, Cal. We aren't going to live happily ever after. This story you had in your head about us – about our love – it's over."

Cal grabs her shoulders roughly. "It doesn't have to be."

"Cal, a love story only works if both people believe it. Otherwise, it's a dream. It's time to wake up."

*

"Wake up, Pats." Payton snaps her fingers.

Patricia's eyes open. Carter is gone. Payton sits on the bed, studies her.

"I let myself in. You're fixed. Carter said your body has only one soul now. He wanted someone here when you woke."

"Can I have coffee?" asks Patricia's voice.

While Payton fixes coffee, Patricia studies her body, runs her hands over the smooth flesh. Patricia's lips smile blissfully. Soon, Payton returns with a steaming mug.

Patricia takes a sip. "Can I have sugar, Payton?"

"Really? Since when?"

Patricia's shoulders shrug. "Life can always be a little sweeter."

When Payton returns with the sugar, she begins talking. "I'm just glad you're okay. I can't even imagine what this must have been like. You should consider…"

But Patricia's ears aren't listening. Patricia's fingers drum impatiently on the nightstand.

"What did you think about Cal? Really?"

Frowning, Payton strokes Patricia's face. "He was okay, but I agree with you. Sometimes you're better off being alone, than with the wrong person. Why?"

"It doesn't matter, does it? Then and now, I suppose. But speaking of solitude, Payton, I'm fine. You don't need to stay."

"Everything okay, Pats?"

"Why?"

"Usually, you call me Paypal."

"Right. I'm fine, Paypal. In fact, I think I'll be happy ever after." Patricia's arms cross over her chest, hands cupping her shoulders. Her hands slide down her front, fall into her lap. "I'd just like to be alone with myself right now. I've missed me."

Hungry Like the Moon

I wake up to the noise of zombies moaning. Sounds like a breeze gliding through a broken seashell.

I'm trapped in a cramped diner with seven zombies: three men, three women, and a little girl. The seven zombies are a mess of torn flesh, bite marks, and gashes. Their flesh is pale, and their eyes are horribly dull – like rotten egg yolks left out in the sun. I've woken up in plenty of bad situations, but this is the worst.

I try to sit up, but can barely move.

The diner is a long, skinny rectangle cut in half lengthways by a bar top. Behind the bar is what's left of a greasy spoon kitchen. The walls are covered with gore, claw marks, and matted hair – evidence of an unquenchable hunger. A horizontal strip of mirror runs along the diner's side and rear walls, most of it now shattered, cracked, or splattered with blood. At the rear of the diner is a short hallway with a unisex bathroom and a boarded exit. The front is simply a door and a window, both reinforced with broken tables.

One of the zombies locks eyes with me, and I know then that my time has come. Before dying, the zombie was a man named Chef. I met him just last night, when he reluctly offered me shelter.

Apparently, that was his last mistake.

*

Last night.

The sun was already low in the sky when I found the diner.

I'd just gotten into town, hopeful that Brooklyn would have a rescue center or shelter for survivors. It'd been three weeks since the zombie outbreak, since the moon had been a waning crescent. I'd spent most of that time tracking my daughter, Melanie, after discovering that her mother, my ex, had been killed. Melanie's trail took her through multiple survivor camps in Ohio, Pennsylvania, and now here, in Brooklyn. It was a trail of desperation and fear. As recently as a few days ago, Melanie fled with a group of survivors to the Big Apple.

Brooklyn was worse than I'd imagined. The streets were filled with abandoned cars, dead animals, the crumbled remains of toppled buildings, and a mix of abandoned possessions: clothing, television sets, high-end jewelry. I imagine those first nights, there'd been a lot of looting – before everyone realized how out of control our world was going to become. Before gasoline and shotgun shells became more valuable than diamonds and cash.

Less than an hour into my walk downtown, a pack of zombies – more than I'd ever seen gathered in one place – started chasing me through the city. I was faster than them, but they were everywhere, cutting me off at every corner. There were hundreds of them, in varying states of decay and dress. A businessman missing an ear. A rotted corpse wearing a blue dress covered in mud and maggots. A teenager in a Twilight t-shirt missing an arm.

When I saw the diner, I knew that people were in there. It wasn't just the thick wood covering the window or the single word spray-painted on the front of the building:

HELP

No, it wasn't just that. I could smell them.

I pounded on their front door, screaming for help. "Please. Please let me in. They're after me. Oh, God. Don't let me die."

Behind the barricaded door, a man and a woman about whether or not to let me inside, though I couldn't tell who was taking which side.

"Please," I begged. "I'm just trying to find my daughter."

When the door finally opened, it wasn't hard to tell who was arguing in my favor and who was against. A tall man with thick forearms and wild curly hair had a shotgun leveled at my heart. Next to him stood a fit woman, probably in her thirties, with a fashionable haircut and exhausted eyes. She pushed the shotgun aside and pulled me into the diner.

"Knock it off, Chef," she said. "We're in this together. It's us against them. If we don't stick together, we're going to lose." She turned her attention to me, offered her hand. "I'm Abbie."

Aside from Chef and Abbie, the only other occupants of the diner were two women, two men, and a little girl.

Chef placed the shotgun in the corner and looked me up and down. "You got any food?" he asked. I shook my head. "What about ammo? I'm guessing that's too much to ask."

I shook my head.

Abbie led me to the rear of the diner and introduced me to the rest of the crew. The two women were likely a couple. I can't remember either of their names; I've never been much good with names, or people for that matter.

Abbie introduced the little girl, Gail, last. The child was tied down to a bed made out of two booths nested together.

Inside my skull, I heard a growl.

The child was pale and sweaty. A blood-stained bandage made from a kitchen apron was wrapped around her forearm. Her eyes were pale as the full moon. I'd seen this before. She'd been bitten, and she was going to turn. Soon, by the looks of it.

"And this is my niece, Gail," said Abbie. She held up a hand, as if to block what I was about to say. "Don't say it. I know. She's going to become one of them soon. I'm not a fool. I know the situation. But before I lose her forever, I'm going to make the most of the time we have left."

"And after that?"

She held up a shiny handgun and her face became a mask of resignation. "After that, I'll put a bullet in its head."

*

It's morning now, and the seven zombies shuffle toward me. Little Gail is the most hideous of all, the front of her tiny dress covered in blood and a huge chunk of flesh missing from her neck. When she moans, her neck makes a hideous whistle.

I stand up slowly, staggering backward. I try to scream, but I can't. It's like my throat is stuffed with gauze.

What comes out instead is a howling moan, the sound of a large dead tree creaking in the wind. At the sound of my moan, the seven zombies cock their heads. Their blue lips fall back over their grey teeth, and their dull yellow eyes drift away.

I take an awkward step forward, and the zombies shuffle away, giving me space. Now's my chance. I take another step, trying to sprint for the front door. But my joints creak like rusty hinges and my muscles feel like play-doh. I fall face-first onto the floor, and my eyes catch my upside-down reflection on a bent spoon.

Staring back at me are two dull yellow eyes.

I'm one of them.

I stand up and stare at the strip of mirror on the wall. Shake my head. Dammit. I'd only wanted to find Melanie. I place a hand over my chest. No heartbeat. Instead, there's an emptiness. A void.

And my heart, it's just rotting inside me.

*

Last night.

My heart quivered as I stepped onto the diner's roof. I needed to get out of here, far away from these good people before the change came. I was plotting my escape when the smell of cigarette smoke distracted me. Sharp teeth bit into my urgency and tugged it to the back of my skull.

Abbie stood on the roof's edge, a cigarette held at her side. She looked at me. Her lopsided grin was like a crescent moon. That wicked smile in the sky that yawns open into an unblinking, laughing eye. I shuddered.

The rooftop offered a beautiful view of the city. Nearby, an old church thrust its steeple into the sky. In the distance stood the Statue of Liberty. I half-expected the statue to be moaning and staggering into the water. Below, the zombies moaned and pounded futilely against the diner's reinforced door. Abbie flicked ash at them lazily.

"The odd thing is, I can't hate them," she said. "As much as I want to, I can't. They're just pathetic and hungry. I can't fault them for that." She holds up her cigarette. "I can't smoke up here during the day. Chef's worried that I'd be spotted. But at night, I can go through two packs. I'm as bad as they are."

In my skull, claws paced restlessly, clacking on bone.

I shook my head. "No, you're not."

"Do you know what I obsess about, when I'm not thinking about Gail? I think about running out of cigarettes. How lame is that?"

I shrugged. "You've got a beast inside you. It's hungry and wants fed, no matter how much it might hurt you in the process. The only way to make the beast go away is to starve it, but that doesn't always work. You can tie it in chains or lock it in a cell, but deep down you know the beast will always find a way out. So, you just do your best. You try to make it through the day."

"Sounds like you speak from experience."

I shrugged and tapped my skull. "I've got my share of monsters in here."

"You know, this probably isn't the safest place in the city," said Abbie, tapping her heel on the roof. "I mean, now you're locked in here with a monster."

If only she'd known.

"I've been in worse spots," I said. "Believe me."

"So, how old is your daughter?"

"She's sixteen. Melanie's a survivor. I've been following her almost since the outbreak. Do you know... Are there any other groups of survivors here in the city?"

She shrugged. "Mostly everyone left during the Evacuation, but we've heard noises at night, over near Park Slope."

I nodded.

"How'd you and your daughter get separated?"

"I haven't seen her since before the outbreak. Her mother and I, we had some issues that couldn't be resolved. Mostly my fault. So, I left. I was out West when the outbreak started. By the time I got back to Ohio, Mel was gone. And her mother... her mother was one of those things."

Abbie patted my shoulder. "I'm sorry."

"Don't be. Death is just a fact of life."

She shook her head sadly. "Not anymore."

*

It takes me a moment to get my bearings. Just like the other undead, I sway gently. My first step is right into a chewed-up wad of flesh on the floor. Why is it familiar?

I stomp and scrape my foot against the floor, trying to get the tissue off of my boots. Again, I lose balance and crash into the floor.

The zombies wander around aimlessly, bumping into tables, knocking chairs against the floor. Somehow, I'm different than them. My thinking is slower than usual, like I'm trying to run underwater, but at least I'm still thinking. Where they seem to be acting on instinct, I still have my capacity to reason, to apply logic.

Zombie Chef pounds at the same door. He's clueless, utterly clueless about how to get out of here. All seven of them are clueless. Abbie is clawing at the wall, scratching off specks of dried blood. Amazingly, despite being dead, her haircut still looks pretty good. The other zombies mill about, occasionally breaking something or falling down – often both at the same time.

Staggering across the room, I make my way to the front door

and gently shove Chef aside. He moans in protest, but doesn't resist.

I pick up the hammer after several tries. My hands are numb, like I've had a shot of Novocain in each finger and am wearing thick wool mittens. Grunting and growling, I manage to slip the claw of the hammer between the wood and the door. I push against the door, and the wood groans.

The noise is exactly the same as the feeling that's growing in my gut: a horrible emptiness worming its way through the soil of my insides. A hunger unlike anything I've ever felt. It burns like a dull grey fire in my gut, its flames licking through my entire body.

By the time I break through the front door, I'm almost blind with hunger. I stagger into the crisp morning air, sniffing madly.

I catch a vague scent and follow it down the street. My seven zombie companions follow after me, moaning and grunting. Maybe they can sense that I'm different than them. Smarter. Superior.

The alpha male of the pack.

*

Last night.

When Abbie and I came back downstairs, Gail's breathing was shallow and raspy. Like somebody sharpening a knife. Her eyes rolled back into her head, and her limbs contorted languidly.

Abbie fiddled with her gun, agonizing over when to pull the trigger. Chef remained slumped by the front door, his gaze shifting between the street and Gail. It was clear that Chef was preparing to make Abbie's decision for her. A nasty triangle of tension swelled between the three of them – Abbie, Gail, and Chef – and the rest of us didn't dare to interfere.

When the tension snapped, it wasn't Abbie, Gail, or Chef responsible; it was me.

Rather, it was the Wolf.

When I stood up, I could already feel the full moon pulling at my marrow and blood. Panic rose on a lake of sweat on the back of my neck. It was too early. The moon couldn't be up yet...

Damn it. The Wolf had tricked me again. The closer we get to moonrise, the more the Wolf is able to exert itself over me. Manipulate me. Make me forget things. I'd had every intention of going up on the roof when the change came, of locking myself up there, but now it was too late. The Wolf was punishing me for all those nights I'd contained it. For all those times the Wolf had emerged only to find itself locked up or bound by chains.

A coat of fur simmered beneath my skin. I fell to the floor screaming, my mouth full of chalk and broken glass. My teeth were rearranging themselves; four fangs digging out of my gums. Blood spilled from my fingertips as thick claws forced themselves through my tender skin.

If there's anything in this world that I loathe more than myself, it's the damn Wolf.

The Wolf consumed me, as it did every full moon night. It ate me from the inside out, its wild animal hunger gnashing and tearing at my insides. At least, that's how it felt.

Abbie knelt to examine me, but then screamed. I growled back, baring my fangs. Soon, the diner was filled with screams and shouts, and then with gunfire.

Wouldn't you know it, not a damn one of them had any silver bullets.

It was a feeding frenzy. Those fools had that diner locked up so tight, there was no way they could escape. One of the lesbians made a break for the rooftop stairs, and I tore out her stomach, left her lying in front of the stairwell door, effectively blocking it. I attacked Chef next, who blew a chunk out of my shoulder with his shotgun. Even as I tore his throat out, I felt a familiar tingle in my shoulder, as the muscle, bone, and skin stitched itself back together.

I can't remember much of what happened next, just that the Wolf slaughtered them all and saved Gail for last, like dessert. After all, she was tied down, going nowhere. When I tore out her throat, the flesh tasted like bad milk.

After that, a fuzzy blanket of white light enclosed my consciousness, and the Wolf took over completely. I'm fairly certain that this blanket of light is what keeps me from going insane. If I had to experience every horror committed by the Wolf, I'd easily lose my mind. It's some built-in function of the Wolf's affliction, putting my mind in isolation while the Wolf runs free.

The last thing I saw before the Wolf took over is the lump of diseased flesh that I spat upon the ground.

*

We shuffle east for several apocalyptic blocks along Atlantic Avenue, gathering a few stray zombies in our wake. I follow the scent of human flesh to a cheap hotel. The front door of the hotel is missing, torn from its hinges. I charge inside, ready to feed the hunger, but soon find only disappointment. The elevators in the lobby are shut down, and the only stairwell is barricaded by a pile of dirty mattresses and broken dressers. It's passable, but it'd take a lot of time and make a lot of noise to get through. I'm about to moan in rage, but then an insight snags at my thoughts.

Any kind of quality shelter will have one main entrance, but also a reliable backdoor.

I stop and let my mind chew on that thought. It seems important, relevant to the situation at hand. Grunting, I stagger back outside and glance down the narrow alley running next to the building. That's when I see what I'm looking for: a fire escape. Someone has arranged a pile of bricks on the fourth level of the fire escape, which extends downward to the second floor. There, the extension ladder has been removed, replaced with a handmade rope ladder.

It's a good system. The people inside can use the fire escape for offense, dropping brick bombs on any zombies nearby. They can also use the rope ladder defensively to escape. But the humans have left it unguarded. Foolish.

My dim-witted colleagues follow me into the alley. I shove Chef against the brick wall and make several awkward attempts to climb onto his shoulders. He stares back at me with a wounded, dumb expression and collapses under my weight. When that doesn't work, I start to shove a dumpster underneath the fire escape. The others catch on eventually. Or more likely they're just imitating me. Finally, we get the dumpster into position.

I shove the female zombie couple up onto the dumpster, point upward and grunt until they climb onto the fire escape. Since the bricks are on the fourth floor landing, I'm assuming that's where our breakfast lives. I wait until the girls are on the third floor before heading back to the front lobby.

When I get to the stairwell entrance, I can already hear broken glass, screams, and gunfire from the fourth floor. Just as I suspected, a few of the humans – perhaps the weakest of the herd – are the first to try to escape, rather then stand their ground. I'm in perfect position to attack when the stairwell door opens.

It's Melanie.

Mel. Even though it's only been a few months since I left, she looks so much older. Her hair is still dyed pink, but is now pulled into a simple braid. Gone is the lip ring and other jewelry. Her normally pale face, once so much like a full moon, is now tanned and dirty. I reach out to hug her, the following words on my lips: Honey, I missed you so much. I'm so glad you're okay. Except what comes out is a rattling moan.

She takes a step backward, holds up a handgun, and shoots me right in the head.

*

For a long while after the Wolf first got inside me, I thought I could hold on to my family. It wasn't uncommon for my job to send me out of town on business, so I made sure that I was always away during the full moon. But then my asshole brother decided to get married during the day of a full moon, which screwed up all my plans.

I went to the wedding, a fairly small affair. Mel, she was one of the bridesmaids. I remember staring at her across the aisle as the minister read the vows to my brother's bride.

Do you take this man to have and to hold...

Later, I gave the toast at the reception, a swanky golf club nearby. I danced with my wife and daughter, and drank a lot of wine. I was in the bathroom when the change came. I stared at myself in the mirror, a look of surprise on my face. And then, my eyes. They were laughing at me. The Wolf was laughing. The damn beast had tricked me, let me lose track of time. As hair slid out of my flesh, I climbed out the window and ran across the well-manicured lawn.

...for better or for worse in sickness and in health...

I woke up the next morning wearing only a pair of tattered tuxedo pants. Next to me was a dead girl in a bridesmaid dress. My heart squeezed into a fist. I knew it had to be Mel. Imagine my relief when I turned over the bloody corpse and found one of the other bridesmaids.

...as long as you both shall live?

The Wolf had sent me a message. It let me know that no one is safe. After that, I left town, vowing never to return.

*

So, that's it. I should be dead, right? Everyone knows that the one way to kill a zombie is to shoot it in the head.

Except I'm okay.

The bullet tears easily through my skull, and suddenly I've lost binocular vision. My little girl shot out my left eye.

It sounds like a light bulb shattering when the bullet exits out the back of my skull. I fall backward, more from surprise than from the impact.

Some of the other zombies must have followed me from the alley, because Mel is now surrounded, firing her gun until it clicks uselessly. She shoots down all but two zombies, a pregnant woman in a sundress and a fit Latino wearing only a wifebeater, who have cornered her behind an ATM machine. My daughter screams as the zombies grab her, tearing the sleeve off of her blue t-shirt.

Next, she whimpers in surprise as I snap the zombies' heads back and slam them head-first onto the lobby floor. I then stomp their heads one after another until my heels are covered with skull and rotten brains.

When it's done, the only sound is Mel's sharp breathing. No, wait. Something's squirming inside pregnant zombie's bloated stomach. Ever so faintly, I can hear something toothless trying to eat its way out.

I already feel a tingle where my eye used to be. It's coming back.

"Daddy?" says Mel.

It's the first time she's called me that since puberty slapped her in the face. I want so much to hug her, but can't be that close to her. If I touch her, the hunger will consume me. And I will consume her.

So instead, I nod and wave her away. On my way back to the stairwell, I stop and kick her gun over to her. Hopefully she has more bullets. At the stairwell door, I turn and blow her a kiss. Grunt.

She whispers to me. "Thank you, Daddy."

*

Walking upstairs, I feel like I'm shedding skin. Walking away from Mel is like a new beginning for me. I'm leaving humanity behind. I'm becoming something new. Part of a new family, where I'm the strongest and smartest. The alpha male.

When I make my way to the hotel room on the fourth floor, it's already covered in blood and gore. The two women are sharing the entrails of an overweight black man. Abbie and Gail are gnawing at an elderly woman's face and hands. Chef has his own victim, a goth chick with lip piercings and multi-colored tattoos covering her chest and arms. She watches in horror as Chef tears out her intestines, gnawing at the pulpy flesh. I fall next to her, pushing Chef away. He growls under his breath and crawls into the corner, taking her intestines with him. The tangled mess of her insides unravels out of her stomach.

I tear off the remains of her shirt. Her left breast is covered with a bright tattoo of a lunging tiger. I bite into her chest, catching the tiger by the tail. She screams, gurgles, chokes, and shudders. I swallow.

It occurs to me then that I've been eating people for years, and it's always been a very lonely pursuit, something that I've never clearly remembered. But now, it feels so good to share the experience. All around me, my gang of zombies moans and bites and grunts. The room is filled with the sounds of squishing, biting, tearing, and swallowing.

It's a feeding frenzy.

As I gnaw on the goth's face, it occurs to me that biting Gail must have been what turned me into a zombie. It makes sense, if you think about it. If a zombie bites you, you eventually become one of them. Likewise, if you bite a zombie, you eventually become a zombie.

But if you're a werewolf who bites a zombie?

Near as I can figure, the lycanthropy disease and the zombie virus must have somehow blended together, putting me in my current state. When I become the Wolf – rather, when the Wolf forces itself out of me – my mind, maybe even my soul, gets shut down. It's like the Wolf puts my core essence in isolation, so that the Wolf can do whatever it wants. It's that isolation that has kept me from going insane over the years. But now, that isolation that has kept my personality and thoughts intact.

I'm a zombie with a werewolf's healing abilities.

I'm practically invincible.

I've got my mind, an unstoppable body, and the world is mine to conquer. But what of the Wolf? My skull is silent. If the Wolf is in there, it's being quieter than ever. Is it possible? Am I cured?

It's almost dusk by the time we finish eating. Soon, the moon will sit all bloated in the sky, staring down at me with its unblinking eye. What will it see?

*

When I lead my pack outside, bloated on fresh meat, I gaze into the sky. Apprehension squirms in my gut. Or maybe it's just maggots.

The moon sits low in the sky behind some buildings, pregnant with possibilities.

And nothing happens.

I'm cured. That wolf that has plagued me for more than a lifetime is gone, driven out of my body by the zombie plague. That damn beast is the reason that I couldn't live a normal life, and now I'm free of it forever. And by forever, I mean forever.

I'm beyond death. Beyond life.

I raise my fist to the sky and moan – a ragged, contemptuous noise.

Behind me, my fellow zombies echo my sentiment. At least, that's what I think at first. They're certainly making a lot of noise, but when I turn around, they've fallen to the pavement. Their dull yellow eyes are glowing in the moonlight. Jagged fangs split rank gums. Grey fur slides out of blue skin. Chipped nails extend from filthy fingertips.

It's the little girl, Gail, who attacks me first, lunging and biting at my thigh. Following her lead, the rest of the zombie werewolves leap upon me, knocking me to the ground. Abbie and Gail snarl and moan over my chest, tearing at my neck. Soon, their muzzles are covered with thick, black blood. Chef tears at my abdomen. The rest gnaw at my arms and legs.

The wolves consume me. It takes them most of the night, but they manage to eat most all of me: fingers, legs, intestines, lungs, and so on. They leave only the upper chest and head.

The worst part? I'm perfectly awake through the whole ordeal. All I can do is watch and wait for them to finish. Every few bites, one of them locks eyes with me, and I can see the Wolf staring back. Those pale glowing eyes are laughing at me.

By the time the sky starts to lighten, Gail leads the pack back inside the hotel. By this point, I'm just a head, a neck, and a few chunks of spine. I'm stuck in the gutter, and all I can do is moan.

I wait for the tingle that tells me I'm healing, but it doesn't come. Maybe I've sustained too much damage. Maybe only my head is protected. I don't know, but I've got a long time to think about it. More than a lifetime.

Already, dull white flames of hunger flicker and spark inside my remains. The hunger threatens to consume me, but it can't. If only it could, but it can't. Instead, it rages in my phantom belly, torturing me.

I moan and moan some more. As if answering my call, Gail appears in the doorway of the hotel. She's just a regular zombie now; the Wolf has retreated. She stares at me and cocks her head. She has something in her hand. What is it? A scrap of food for me, perhaps? She holds it up into the morning light, and I can see that the little girl is holding my daughter's torn sleeve.

Gail holds the sleeve to her nose and sniffs.

Her eyes are smiling.

And Then, the Hole

Lara stands over the hole, a gaping wound in the dirt floor of her grandma's basement. She has an unlit cigarette and—according to her watch—exactly one hour and twenty-five minutes of pure freedom. Her son's napping upstairs. Grandma's out prowling through yard sales. This is Lara's one moment of the day, possibly of the week, all for herself. A half-read Rick Hautala novel and a tub of chocolate peanut butter ice cream wait for her upstairs. Yet all she can think about is this hole.

It's about the width of a manhole cover. Something about the way it yawns open reminds her of a baby bird's beak stretched wide for a bit of chewed-up worm. She drops to her knees and sniffs. The void below stinks of rich dirt and pulpy vegetables, like compost from a garden. Even down here, she can smell hints of the lake.

"Fuck," she says.

On her way to the stairs, she kicks the useless punching bag slumped in the corner. Her handwraps dangle unused nearby. She nods at her reflection in the full-length mirror that she uses for shadowboxing. Punching at shadows is fine but sometimes she needs to hit something. Hard. She stomps upstairs and follows the dog outside.

Sunshine warms her face. She lights her cigarette but can barely taste it. She exhales a lazy cloud, soon ushered away by a breeze off of Lake Ontario. The smell of the lake—dead fish and sour water— always makes her yearn for Florida. She and her son are better off here in Oswego, New York, but she craves that salty air. The promise of the ocean. Loud music. Late nights. A tide to wash everything away and start anew. In Florida, the past was buried under sparkling sand and a fresh tide. Here, history forms a thick crust over everything, threatening to smother the present. Brick roads. Slate sidewalks. Grandma told her several times about how the town housed Holocaust survivors after World War II. Well before that,

Oswego served as the final stop on the Underground Railroad for escaped slaves heading north to Canada.

Nearby, the heavy bag stand slouches in the grass. It's a metal frame with two wide feet. Like a sea serpent, it has a long, tall neck with a hook for mounting a punching bag. She bought it on a whim two weeks ago at a church yard sale. It watches her smoke, taunting her with its emptiness.

She drops the cigarette and grinds it into the grass. She wraps the butt inside a Reese's cup wrapper and hides it in the trash bin. The cats wait for her at the back door.

"Come on, Charlie," she says to the terrier mix standing in the backyard.

The dog stays under a bush and tilts his head. Ears flop. He's been acting strange since yesterday. Since she found the hole.

"Charlie, come on." She won't raise her voice. It's naptime.

Behind her, a cat meows. Charlie growls.

The noise crawls under her skin. She had the nightmare again last night, the same one that's haunted her for years. She's running through a dark cemetery. Moisture covers the grass. The tombstones glisten, their sweaty marble faces carved not with dates and names but with random snippets of song. *Safe from pain and truth and choice. And other poison devils.* A pack of wolves chases after her—shaggy puppets of the shadows that drench the graveyard. She hears them gaining on her. Harsh breaths. Mournful howls. Claws scraping marble. *You're pulling us and dragging us down this dead end road.* Sometimes they catch her. Jaws like iron vises clamp onto her calves. The thing is, getting caught isn't the worst part.

"Fine, stay out there," she says, resisting the urge to slam the door. "Fuck."

She strokes one of the cats and listens to the baby monitor. It offers only a slight hiss. She checks her watch. It offers an hour and twelve minutes.

Crossing the room, she can't help but pick up her son's blocks, though she knows he'll get right back to them after naptime. She stacks the morning newspaper under the coffee table, even though Grandma's only halfway through the Sudoku.

She washes her hands in the kitchen sink and checks her phone. Rick texted her five minutes ago. "I was wondering if you wanted to go to the farmers market Thursday night and get some dinner. We could watch . . ."

Rick's a nice enough guy, but she knows it won't work. She doesn't bother sliding her thumb across the screen to see the rest of the message. Ninety percent of the guys she meets can't get their eyes above her neck. The other ten percent—Rick included—can't handle dating someone tougher than them.

She opens the basement door. A dark staircase bows at her feet. She grabs the baby monitor and heads downstairs. The hole's waiting for her.

It has been since yesterday.

She and Rick were trying to dig out just a few inches of the dirt floor, enough that her bag stand would fit in the low basement. Her shovel struck a panel of wood. She scraped the dirt away with her shovel, revealing a square of wood about the size of a car window. Rick pried the panel upward. A hole stared back at them.

A chill licked her spine.

"Balls," she said. "What the hell's this?"

Rick shrugged. "Some kind of drainage?"

She shook her head and knelt. "Too big for that. Give me the flashlight."

Her flashlight's beam revealed a cramped passage about as long as she was tall. The void sloped downward at a shallow angle. A rectangle of rusted metal reinforced the ceiling. Bolted to the metal, thin columns of rotted wood braced the walls. It looked like a miniature mineshaft. The packed earth didn't move, but she sensed tension in there. Like a coiled spring.

"We'll have to tear it out," she said.

"No way," Rick said. "I'm not going in there. We don't even know what it is."

"Fine. Then I'll do it."

Rick pointed across the floor. "Just put the bag stand over there."

She shook her head. "It'll block the furnace."

"So?"

"So that's not where I want it."

"Then just hang your bag from the rafters."

"It shakes the whole house when I hit it. It scares my son and agitates the cats."

"Well maybe you should've measured the damn thing before

you bought it."

An argument ensued. Words flew back and forth like an angry ping-pong ball. It ended with four simple words that she'd spoken many times before.

"My life. My rules."

Now, her watch offers her fifty-five minutes. She wiggles down into the hole with a hammer and a flashlight. She goes in headfirst, so that she can pry out the beams at the passage's end. The stink smells like bad breath. The ground bites at her elbows as she shimmies deeper. Exposed roots scrape against her, though she can't imagine what tree owns those roots.

She rolls onto her back and digs in her heels. She scoots deeper. The slope of the passage helps. Gravity does a little of the work. Rocks scrape against her shoulder blades. The low ceiling nudges her breasts.

Her outstretched hand touches the end of the passage. She wedges her hammer's claw into the frame. The wood groans but doesn't budge. Even after she stops exerting pressure, the wood continues to moan. She listens. It can't be the wood making this low murmur. Maybe a plumbing pipe runs past here.

The flashlight blinks out. Her heart simmers.

She taps the flashlight against the dirt. Nothing. She holds her breath. A bit of light filters through the hole from the basement. The dimness offers some reassurance.

"Don't freak out," she whispers. "Just get the job done."

Once her eyes adjust, she pries again at the beams. The wood groans. Bits of dirt fall onto her exposed neck and arms.

Something eclipses the light near her feet. Her eyes claw at total darkness.

"Hello?" she says. "Grandma, is that you?"

Her ears strain. She thinks maybe she hears the static from the baby monitor, but it's probably only her imagination. The wood growls, a ticking noise like a tin can scraped slowly across a rusty saw.

Bits of her nightmare flash in the darkness. Panting breaths. Glistening tombstones. Yellow eyes. Her head reels.

She pushes away from the end of the passage, trying to scoot herself toward freedom. Except gravity has shifted. The hole's gentle slope somehow stretches steeper. Her shoulder muscles ache. Gravity presses her head against the far wall. It feels now like she's in a vertical hole, the weight of her muscular legs shoving down at her. Bits of dirt drop onto her face. Her eyes sting. Other things fall, too. Squirming things. Wiggling things. She swats at her skin, at the shadows, at the walls.

The tunnel contracts. Dirt presses against her chest. She coughs. Sweat turns the dirt to mud, a thin layer of the stuff slathered all over her. She wants more than anything to scream, but she won't give it the satisfaction.

More nightmarish scenes flicker in the dark. Tombstones. Raised hackles. Blistered hands. Endless rows of cotton. These aren't her nightmares, she realizes. They're someone else's memories. Endless days of traveling by moonlight, hiding in barns and cellars. A slave girl spent the night here, her last stop on the Underground Railroad. Her last stop anywhere.

"You'll be safe here," a man's voice said.

"It's dark," the girl replied.

The man just laughed.

The same scene repeats itself over and over with different victims. Scarred dark flesh. Wide eyes. Brave souls who have survived so much, only to have their freedom jerked away.

She realizes that what's jabbing in her back aren't rocks. They're bones.

Anger rages inside her. The tunnel closes in, almost pinning her arms against her. The earth presses, like a throat trying to swallow. With what momentum she can manage, she punches at the dirt. The wood groans. Maybe it laughs. She punches all the harder.

More ghostly scenes flash across her vision. Numbers tattooed across a thin forearm. Skeletal figures dressed in rags. Piles of dead bodies. Gunfire. Freedom. An endless voyage across the ocean. A train ride. Endless weeks behind a chain link fence. Finally, real freedom. And then, the hole.

"Go on," a woman said. "I need you to clean it out."

"It's dark," a young man said with a thick European accent.

"Don't worry. I'll keep the light on."

Except she didn't. And the hole fed on the young man's boundless suffering. It took an eternity to digest it all.

Salty tears. Rusty blood. These scents hang heavy in the dirt-speckled air.

"No," Lara yells.

She punches through the dirt. Her knuckles split against cracked wood. Her muscles strain and flex. Her arms become pistons, punching and elbowing at the hungry tunnel. She pulls against the wooden frame, inching her way to the exit. Something—wood or bone or rock—bites into her thigh. She keeps on fighting.

Fresh air nips at her ankles. A light pierces the darkness. The hole whines at her, an infantile noise that she prays doesn't come from the baby monitor. She slams her fist into the dirt. She thuds her elbow through rotten wood. A few more thrusts later, she sprawls on the dirt floor beside the hole. She rolls away toward the stairs.

According to her watch, she has fifty-two minutes of freedom left, except the hands are frozen in place. Dead as the flashlight. She coughs and takes a breath, gobbling at the fresh air.

Everything seems startlingly normal in the dim basement. The baby monitor hisses static. She rises onto her shaky legs and makes for the stairs. It's over. She's free. She can go upstairs, get her son, and leave this haunted place—this hungry hole—forever.

Her reflection's waiting for her in the mirror. She takes a good look at herself. Torn knuckles. Scraped, bruised flesh. Torn pants. Covered in mud. She takes her handwraps off the wall and winds the cotton cloth across her knuckles. First her left hand, then the right. Blood soaks through the pale fabric. She grabs another hammer off the pegboard, pauses, and takes a pry bar, too.

She walks across the room and falls to her knees beside the hole. As she wiggles back inside, her nightmare echoes in her mind. The worst part isn't the cemetery or the wolves. It's not getting bit or falling down. No, the unbearable part is the running away.

The hole growls around her. The shadows grit their teeth. She rears back her fist.

The Harm

Morning

Collin sprinkles a dash of salt on the square napkin on the bar. After pouring himself an almost cold beer, he takes a sip and places it on the napkin.

Something behind the bar catches his eye – one of those tear-away daily calendars. It's still set on September 17th, the day of the zombie outbreak. Collin takes another drink and rips at the pages until he hits December 31st. He tears that page off, too, and then with a thick magic marker writes today's date:

MARCH 17
ST PADDYS DAY

Someone jostles the trashcan propped outside the front window – the only entrance to the fortified pub aside from the metal doors in the basement leading to the side alley. Must be one of the Harm's other tenants, probably too excited to sleep, too.

The first floor of the Harmony Lake Apartment Building, known by its tenants since the outbreak as *the Harm*, was until recently a diner. Over the past few weeks, Collin has worked almost non-stop converting that diner into a pub. The countertop was easily converted to a bar, but the other details – neon bar lights, a keg of beer, various liquors – had to be scavenged from bars and residences in the greater Cleveland area. The pub's windows and doors are boarded and bricked over, except for the front window resting at shoulder height on the wall.

Collin finishes his beer, pours a new one into a fresh glass, and jogs with it to the window. "Looks like the first toast of the day is yours to make," he announces, leaning out the windowsill into the pre-dawn chill.

But looking back at him isn't a neighbor. It's a zombie.

Before dying, the zombie was a young man, probably a senior in high school. A flap of skin hangs loose from his skull over a face still sneering with youthful arrogance. The zombie grabs Collin's wrist and the beer falls to the ground, showering broken glass and beer onto the sidewalk.

The zombie lurches forward to bite. Collin's first instinct is to pull backward, but he knows better. The zombie's grip is too tight, and it only takes one bite to get converted. So he shoves himself through the window, tackling the zombie.

They fall in a heap, and Collin punches the zombie in the nose. Its head snaps backward against the concrete, and Collin holds its head down. Its mouth snaps open and closed, open and closed. As the zombie struggles, Collin's fingers slide into its head wound. The skull is cool as a stone.

A glint catches Collin's eye... a long shard of broken glass. In one smooth motion, he releases the zombie's head, grabs the shard of glass, and drives it into the zombie's eye socket, just as the zombie tries to bite. By the time the glass pierces the zombie's brain, its teeth are already on Collin's forearm. But instead of biting, the zombie shudders and goes limp.

Doesn't get much closer than that.

Collin wipes his hands on the zombie's clothes and discovers that the glass shard has cut his palm. He'll need to put a bandage on his hand, just as soon as he erases any indication of what happened.

He drags the zombie into the adjacent alley, which is just wide enough for a car. Above is the rusty fire escape that the tenants use to access the Harm's upper floors. In more prosperous times, each of the apartment complex's seven floors was its own full apartment. But as the neighborhood declined, the owner segmented each floor into two separate apartments, providing twice as many renters. As a result, only half of the apartments actually have access to the fire escape. Not really a big deal, since the fire escape is an antiquated, rusty mess.

The zombie is easily concealed under a pile of trash. Collins looks up at the fire escape, making sure no one's looking. If folks learn about the zombie, they'll call off the holiday.

He can just hear Henry now...

*

"It's too dangerous," said Henry.

This was last month, during one of sessions they've informally dubbed "town meetings." Always held late at night after Bill and Barbara's kids were asleep, the town meetings were located on the second floor, where all the interior walls were knocked out to make a Commons area. There, all the windows were heavily boarded, even the one opening up to the fire escape. The Commons is the only place in the building where lights could be used after dark. It still smelled faintly of drywall even though it'd been weeks since they cleared out all the interior walls. Since the suicides.

Collin had just proposed that the survivors make a concerted effort to celebrate St. Patrick's Day, and of course, Henry had shot it down.

"It's not too dangerous," said Collin. "Zombie sightings are way down."

"That's true," said KC, the beauty in 6B with a café au lait complexion and long black hair. Collin smiled at her, trying not to stare for too long.

KC continued. "How long has it been since a zombie has even been near the Harm?" *The Harm* is what the tenants have been calling Harmony Lake since the outbreak.

"We saw one three days ago," said Simon from 7A, a lean man with stylish hair. Charles, his partner, nodded in confirmation.

Henry folded his arms over his chest. "We can't let our guard down." He's not a big man, but everything he says sounds like an ordinance.

Collin was ready for this. He'd practiced all day in a mirror. "Henry, you know I respect you, man. I'm the first to admit that if not for you, we'd be out in the streets trying to eat each other."

That was entirely true. In the first days of the undead outbreak, Henry had mobilized the apartment building tenants, first by disabling the elevator and then by destroying the first flight of stairs – effectively cutting the building off from the undead. A veteran of the Gulf War, Henry designed the water catchers to store rainwater, led the scavenging teams to find canned food, and trained everyone on basic self-defense and survival.

Collin continued: "You taught us how to survive, Henry, and I'm grateful for that. But it's been five months, man. Survival isn't good enough anymore. We need to live. We need something to look forward to, brother. People are burning out. We busted our asses for months turning this building into a fortress, but now people are getting bored, antsy."

"Amen," said Collin's upstairs number in 4B, Pork Chop, whose real name was Steve.

"Boredom," said Mr. John, the substitute elementary school teacher from 4A, "is just a lack of imagination."

Collin ignores them both. "We need something to celebrate, man. We passed on Thanksgiving. Fine, it's not like we had the food for a big feast. We passed on Christmas. Understandable, the kids were afraid the zombies would follow Santa down the chimney. We passed on New Year's, because the city was overrun with looters. Great. And this week, we passed on Valentine's Day. That made sense. Many of us have lost loved ones; no need to rub salt in that wound. But we can't pass on St. Patrick's Day. It's the last good holiday of the year."

"What about Easter?" asked Marlene from 3B, an artist who keeps mostly to herself.

Collin waved his hand dismissively. "Who gives a shit about Easter? And really, do we want to be celebrating resurrection? Isn't fuckers coming back from the dead what put us in this predicament in the first place?"

"There's no need to swear," said Mr. John.

"What about the kids?" said Barbara from 6A. "What are the kids supposed to do while we're getting drunk all day?"

"The same thing they usually did," said her ex-husband Bill, the balding, middle-aged father from 5A, "whenever you had one of your..." He makes quotes with his fingers. "...lost days."

Just as Bill and Barbara are about to launch into a fight, derailing the entire conversation, Henry's daughter Constance broke in. "It's no big deal," she said. "I'll watch them."

Collin hadn't even realized Constance was here. Neither did Henry, judging by his expression. Time for Collin to play his trump card, while Henry was taken off-guard.

"Henry, man. How many have we lost since New Years? How many suicides?"

That was a low blow, and Collin knew it.

"Collin's right," said KC. "We need this." She stared coldly at Henry, and Collin could almost taste the tension between them. "People need more out of life than survival; we need passion. Without passion for living, we'll all fall apart."

Henry shook his head, but he wasn't disagreeing. He was just expressing his distaste for the whole affair. "Fine. Do what you want. But don't blame me if it blows up in your faces."

*

KC puts on her face, a deep red lipstick and eye shadow with a hint of green. After sliding into a pair of jeans and a drab green sweater, she starts to ponytail her hair, but realizes that she cut her hair short last night.

The entire time she'd been with Henry, he'd urged her to cut her hair. "You might as well just be wearing a zombie handle on the back of your head," he'd said.

She loved brushing and braiding her hair, but in truth, she'd kept her hair long because it was her link to the old life. But last night, she cut her hair short in a fit of… boredom? Or maybe rage? Angry boredom?

She spins around in front of her mirror, admiring herself. She had to give Henry credit. The workout regimen he'd designed – squats, pushups, clean-and-presses, jumping jacks – has paid off. She looks better now than when she was a dancer, flashing her skin on stage for tips.

People always say they can't imagine how she could take her clothes off in front of a crowd. And KC always replies that her theatre background prepared her well for the job. When she was on stage, she was playing a part. She was the Temptress. Her motivation? To use men's lust to fill her pockets, or g-string.

The first weeks after the zombie outbreak, she played a different role: the Survivor. Her motivation? To do whatever it took.

In those early weeks, she and Henry had formed a tight partnership. She'd even bonded with Henry's teenage daughter, Constance. But she soon learned that Henry was only interested in the Survivor, not in the real KC.

Back in late December, Mr. Parker in 2A had slit his wrists in the night. When Susie from 2B went to check on him the next morning, Parker had become a zombie. He bit her, and then she turned, too.

Henry and KC had been a couple at the time. After dispatching the two zombies, Henry had yelled to everyone in the building, "The next time one of you cowards decides to off yourselves, use a fucking gun and blow out your brains. Think of it as a common courtesy."

That night, a shot rang out from 5B, the apartment below her and Henry's. Mr. Tyler had killed himself. She and Henry had been making love when it happened. The following morning, KC moved out of Henry's apartment in 6B and back into her own in 7B.

Now, as KC leaves her apartment, she knows her motivation for today's party: to show Henry what he's been missing.

Stepping into the stairwell, she runs into Barbara from 6A. Barbara has on a lime green dress, perfect with her reddish brown hair. She's in her thirties, with a perky soccer mom look.

"I love your hair," says Barbara.

"Thanks. It was a sudden impulse last night."

"You heading down?"

KC nods. "Want to go down together?"

Barbara shakes her head. "I need to check in on Connie and the kids first."

This doesn't surprise KC; she's always gotten major disapproval vibes from Barbara, probably because Barbara doesn't want KC to be a bad influence on her three kids.

Barbara's kids had been visiting their dad Bill for the weekend when the outbreak started. Somehow, Barbara had managed to fight her way to the building during the height of the outbreak. She lived with Bill for a few weeks, and folks wondered if they might get back together. But she moved out by the end of October, and now the kids are shuffled back and forth every few days between Bill's apartment on the fifth floor and Barbara's apartment on the sixth floor.

"Well, I'll see you down there," says KC. "Tell Constance I said hello."

*

Constance hates parents.

She's now convinced that her dad is never going to leave her in peace.

"And you know what to do if anything goes wrong, right?" asks her father.

Constance holds up the walkie-talkie. "Dad. I got this. Just go and have a good time. Live a little."

She and her father, Henry, stand in the kitchen of Bill's cramped apartment on the seventh floor. She'd only been there five minutes before Dad came knocking to check on her. In the living room, Brenda, Bobbi, and Beth are playing yet another game of Candyland. Someone just drew the ice cream card, and Bobbi is pitching a fit.

"And you have extra batteries for the walkie-talkie?"

"Yeah, Dad. Go get your drink on."

"Don't talk like that, hon."

"Well, that's what you're going to do, right? Get hammered? Snockered? Sauced? Bent?"

"Snockered?" repeats Dad. "If you're not comfortable, Connie, I can stay. I don't mind."

"Dad, it's Constance. Please call me Constance." She pauses, considers. "Are you stalling because KC will be there?"

He hesitates, and Constance knows she nailed it. After reciting a list of rules and guidelines, Dad makes a hasty retreat. Constance runs to the bathroom and starts her makeup, just like KC showed her.

It seemed like an eternity ago that Constance found the cell phone on the fire escape. She'd made a habit of climbing up the fire escape at sunset to watch dusk become night. Then, one night she found a cell phone duct-taped to the railing.

A text message was waiting for her: "MY NAME IS ARTHUR. YOU ARE BEEUTIFUL."

It took her a whole day of internal debate before she responded. In the weeks that followed, she and Arthur texted back and forth several times a day. When the phone battery died, a new one was waiting for her the next night.

And now, today, she'd finally meet Arthur. Their first date.

Someone knocks on the door, and Constance jumps. It's Barbara. Crap. Constance rinses off her face.

*

The tenants are already loud by the time Henry makes it to pub. Too loud.

The first thing Henry notices is the aroma of eggs and ham. He stands in the middle of the pub, impressed. The walls have painted to mimic dark wood paneling. The light fixtures have been converted to intimate candle-lit lamps. Irish-themed paintings and banners adorn the walls. A Guinness mirror, only slightly cracked, hangs behind the bar. Marlene has painted a mural on the front wall depicting a crowded bar scene, making the pub feel larger yet more cramped.

"Henry, my man," says Collin from behind the bar. "What can I get for you?"

"Your gun, to start with." This had been Henry's one non-negotiable about this party. All the handguns would be locked up in his gun safe, which now sits at the end of the bar.

"Okay, folks. Let's lock 'em up," says Henry.

He expects resistance, but everyone's all too happy to be relieved of the heavy responsibility. Once the last gun is locked the safe, Henry pockets the key.

Everyone has a drink in-hand, mostly green beer, and Irish music plays softly over a battery-controlled jukebox. It's a party. An actual party.

For the first time since the zombie outbreak, Henry feels entirely uncomfortable.

He slides up to the bar next to Mr. John, who is eating a plateful of green stuff. Henry sniffs, shakes his head. Collin has used a camping stove to boil water for dehydrated breakfast meals.

"Hey, Sam-I-Am," says Collin. "Would you like green eggs and ham?"

Henry nods. "Uh, sure."

Collin puts a few drops of food coloring into an empty glass, pours Henry a rich green beer.

"You wore green," says Collin, handing Henry the beer.

Henry looks down at his drag green cargo pants and army green t-shirt, his standard outfit most every day. "Green beer. Nice touch."

"The trick," says Collin, leaning across the bar in a conspiratorial whisper, "is to use blue good coloring. The blue mixes with the yellow beer for a perfect green." Collin holds his own beer in the air and announces, "I'd like to make a toast. Here's to the Harm!"

Everyone bellows in response: "To the Harm!"

As Henry sips his beer, he can't help but notice the bandage over Collin's hand. "What did you do to your hand?"

"Oh, you know me," says Collin, taking a mock boxer's stance. "I was fighting a zombie." Henry must have tensed, because Collin laughs and says, "Kidding, man. I cut my hand cleaning up some broken glass. Relax, man. The zombies are long gone."

Afternoon

By midday, the party is in full swing. Collin stands behind the bar, surveying the fruits of his labors. Mr. John and Barbara are dancing at the back of the pub. Pork Chop and Simon are shooting darts. Charles and Bill are talking sports. Marlene and KC are doing shots. Even Henry seems to be having a good time.

Collin wipes the sweat from his brow. He hadn't realized how hard he was working. As he reaches forward to edge up the volume on the radio, he has to steady himself against the bar.

KC drifts down the bar in front of Collin, her smile as wide and carefree and gorgeous as he's ever seen it. "You outdid yourself, Collin. This is great."

"Glad you're enjoying yourself. Can I get you another round?"

"Please."

"I'll put it on your tab." Collin pours another pair of whiskey shots, makes a hash mark next to Marlene's and KC's names on his notepad.

"What's with the tabs?" asks KC. "'Cause if you're billing us, I can't imagine how I'll ever afford all this."

Collin shrugs, wincing at the sudden tightness in his muscles. "I thought it'd make the experience more realistic." This is only half-true. He also wants to monitor how much everyone is drinking. So far, everyone seems sufficiently inebriated.

"You've thought of everything, haven't you?"

"I used to work as a grad student in the alumni office at Case Western. I helped plan a lot of alumni events. It's all about the details."

"Uh-huh."

"See, I look out at everyone having a good time, and it's like I'm stoking this fire, this green fire. I'm just here to help you and the other little green flames consume as much as possible. To burn as bright and as hot as we can for as long as we can."

KC shakes her head. "You play with fire long enough, you'll get burned."

"Maybe, but you can't plan for every possible thing that can go wrong. You just have to be flexible and adapt."

"That's funny," says KC, her gaze shifting across the room to Henry. "Henry said pretty much the same thing about self-defense. You can't have a counter for every possible attack. You just learn to be ready for anything."

She has a wistful look on her face that sends a tremor through Collin's heart. He has two sudden realizations: 1) he orchestrated this entire event to impress KC; and 2) she still has major feelings for Henry.

This is going to be harder than he thought.

*

Constance hates her nose.

She waits in the living room of apartment 5B trying to ignore the faint bloodstain on the wall – all that's left of Mrs. Cooper.

Sighing at her reflection, she tucks her compact mirror into her heavy, bulging purse. Maybe he's not coming. Maybe he's not the brown-haired boy who looked so yummy in he pictures he sent. Constance shivers, imagining some old fart fondling himself while staring at the very evocative pictures she sent to Arthur. Oh, god. She's an idiot. How could she let herself get—

A knock at the window jolts her out of her mental hamster wheel and she looks up, grateful to see the boy whom she'd come to love. Arthur offers her a grin – at once mischievous and warm – and opens the window.

"Constance," he says. "Hi."

"Hi, Arthur."

"Can I come in?"

"Sure. Welcome to the Harm."

He steps through the open window. She'd imagined him lean like a basketball player, but he's more like a rugged soccer player.

"I've been really looking forward to this, Constance."

"Me, too."

She rises from the chair and hugs him awkwardly. He holds her against him – he smells like dust and sweat – and rubs his hands over the small of her back.

"You sure we don't have to worry about the adults?" he asks.

"They're down in the pub, and they will be all day." After a pause, she adds, "And all night."

"And the other kids?"

"They're next door. I bribed the oldest sister."

He squeezes her tighter. "Good."

The moment's perfect until something scrapes against the window. Her first thought is that a zombie has followed Arthur up the fire escape, but then Arthur squeezes her still tighter and says,

"Come on in, guys. We're all clear."

She knows she's screwed. He begins kissing her neck, licking at her perfumed skin. Two more boys enter through the window. A third is still on the fire escape.

For a second, she panics. Blood rushes to her head, and she trembles. But then she recalls Dad's training sessions, and she channels the fear into productive energy.

With perfect timing, her father's voice comes over the walkie-talkie: "Connie, everything okay up there?"

The boys jump at the sound of her father's voice. Constance takes advantage of the distraction and bites Arthur's ear, tearing the lower lobe clean off. He screams and shoves her away, exactly what she wanted him to do. As her momentum carries her backward, she kicks Arthur in the groin. He spills over, his bloody ear sending an arc of blood across the carpet.

"Constance?" says her father.

She falls back over the chair and grabs her purse. Out comes her Kel-Tec .380. She aims the tidy handgun at Arthur's chest and fires. He flies backward with a thud. Next, she shoots the boy on the fire escape. It's not a chest shot, but she wings his shoulder. She fires again, and he spills over the railing. She shoots another boy twice in the back as he's running out of the room.

The front door slams shut, and Constance sprints across the apartment. The last boy ran into the stairwell. Shit. He better not come near the kids. When she enters the stairwell, he's on the stairs, probably heading for the roof.

He sees Constance and holds up his hands in the universal sign for surrender. "Please. Don't shoot."

"Who are you?"

"My name's Tom."

"Why, Tom? Just tell me why."

He's a bit smaller than Arthur, but built like a wrestler.

"We just... we've been on our own for so long. You seem so safe here. We just... we wanted that. Wherever we go, the zombies always find us. Just last night, we lost another—"

"Enough," says Constance. She holds her walkie-talkie to her ear, and calls for her father. "Daddy? Daddy, it's me." But he doesn't respond.

Tom's eyes go wide, his vision focused behind Constance. She sidesteps and turns around. It's Arthur and his friend, their undead eyes glazed, staggering forward. Constance raises her gun, trying to decide which to shoot first. It's then that she realizes she has just one bullet.

So, she shoots Tom in the leg.

*

Henry can barely look at her.

KC is at the bar, tossing back shots with Marlene, her short hair like swirls of dark cream in the lantern light. She's never – ever – looked so beautiful. He's only half-paying attention to whatever Simon and Charles are talking about. Bill's the same way, can barely take his eyes off his ex Barbara and Mr. John over in the corner. They stopped dancing awhile ago, and are now snuggled up close, giggling and flirting at one of the high-backed booths lining the opposite wall. Henry will keep an eye on the situation, in case Bill decides to make a scene.

The air in the pub is starting to get to Henry. He's about to get up when Collin brings him another beer.

"How you doing, Henry?"

"I'm fine."

Collin stands there, studying the empty space between them as if planning his next move during a chess game. "Everything seems to be going pretty well, don't you think?"

"Seems so."

"What do you think of KC's new hair?"

Henry gets off of his stool. "Look, I need a break. I'm going to go upstairs for a bit."

"Actually, would you mind checking the dumps in the basement? We've had a lot of pissing already. I'd hate for the system to overflow."

"Sure," says Henry.

A couple weeks back, Henry helped Collin scavenge some parts from porta-johns at a nearby construction site. They'd modified the existing toilets in the pub's bathrooms so that the waste would collect in the basement. With a bit of sawdust for the smell, the Harm's pub now has two functioning toilets.

He tries not to make eye contact with KC as he walks to the basement stairs.

Downstairs, he uses a flashlight to check on the waste buckets

– way too full. Grabbing a dirty bucket in each hand, he makes his way to the exit stairs leading up to the street level – the pub's only other entrance.

Once in the alley, he's pleased to find a sunny yet chilly day. Maybe he'll go for a quick jog, make sure the surrounding blocks look all clear. But first, he holds his walkie-talkie to his ear.

"Connie," he says. "Everything okay up there?"

She doesn't respond, which is only typical. Feeling the first tingle of adrenaline under his skin, Henry tries again.

"Constance?"

Above, gunshots ring out. Henry puts down the buckets, looks upward. Someone's on the fire escape, possibly Connie.

More gunshots, sounds like there's only one gun. Sounds like Connie's.

He steps back in time to see a bloody teenage boy falling right toward him. Henry sidesteps, but one of the boy's legs catches him in the side of the head.

For a moment, everything's black.

When Henry comes to, the teenager, now a zombie, is biting his neck, tearing out a mouthful of flesh. One eyeball dangling from the zombie's eye socket, resting against Henry's ear. With a grunt, Henry elbows the zombie in the face. After spilling the contents of his pocket onto the ground, Henry finds his knife and stabs it into the zombie's eye.

But he doesn't have time to rest. Something moans down the alley. Another zombie, possibly attracted by the gunshots. And still another. Four more. Struggling to his feet, Henry staggers down the basement stairs. He must secure the door and send the others to help Connie.

He makes it to the basement and locks the exit door before passing out from blood loss. Before the darkness takes him, he has one last thought: the key to the gun safe... he dropped it in the alley.

*

KC would gnaw off her own foot for a cigarette right now. It's been weeks since she quit, but the booze is quickly going to her head. A chalky taste in her mouth begs to be coated in the wooly warmth of smoke.

"What's wrong?" asks Collin, the man with the plan.

"Nothing," she says, then changes her mind. "I want a

cigarette."

This is only half-truth. She's also incredibly horny. It's been weeks since the last time she and Henry did it. He wasn't incredibly inventive in bed, but what he lacked in creativity he made up for with determination.

"I thought you quit," says Collin.

"Yeah, I did, but... Well, you know... I'm half-tempted to smoke one of Simon's nasty cloves."

"No need," says Collin, pulling out an unopened pack of Marlboro Lights, her brand. He taps it against the bar top, then opens the foil and offers her one, takes one for himself. The little darling even has a lighter.

She inhales the smoke into her lungs, and it tastes horrible. But the smoke swirls inside her head, stirs the liquor in her veins.

"Oh my," she says. "That's lovely."

Collin exhales a stream of smoke. "Another drink?"

She shakes her head. "I didn't think you smoked."

"Only on special occasions."

"Yeah," she says. "It's been awhile since we had one of those."

She feels a pang of shame, wonders what Henry will say when he sees her smoking. Not that she cares, of course. Odd, he left awhile ago and hasn't come back.

"I wonder what's keeping Henry."

Collin shrugs. "I'm sure he's fine."

Evening

Collin hears Henry moaning in the basement, but no one else notices. Just to be sure, Collin turns up the music anyway. Clearly agitated about Henry's long disappearance, KC eyes the basement door. If Collin doesn't think of something fast, she's going to storm down there and discover what Collin already knows: Henry is a zombie.

And that would almost certainly ruin the party.

With a flash of inspiration, Collin comes out from behind the bar, holding the wall for support. He'd stopped sweating earlier but has been chilly ever since. What's more, his hearing is suddenly exceptionally acute. He can hear all the dirty things Barbara is whispering to Mr. John.

"I'm going to go help Henry," says Collin. "He can sleep it off in one of the booths."

"Thanks, Collin," says KC, patting his shoulder.

He pauses for a moment to savor her touch. Also, he's stalling.

It's cold, even at the top of the stairs. Putting on his jacket, Collin descends slowly, expecting Henry to lunge out of the darkness. And, of course, that's exactly what happens. Henry reaches from under the exposed stairs, catching Collin's ankle. Already woozy, he loses balance and tumbles down the stairs.

The pain is excruciating – as if his muscles were filled with hardened glue. He tries to get up, but Henry is on him. Teeth press against Collin's neck. He closes his eyes, waiting for the pressure of Henry's bite.

But it never comes.

Henry presses his cold nose against Henry's flesh and sniffs – a deep, congested noise like a rutting pig. Abruptly, Henry loses interest, releases Collin, gets to his feet. Dread squirms in Collin's gut. If Henry won't eat him, that can only mean one thing: Collin is infected. The zombie's blood must have gotten into the cut on his hand this morning. All the alcohol in Collin's body is probably just slowing down the inevitable conversion. He places a hand over his chest; his heart beats sluggishly.

His newfound hearing must be a symptom of the disease. That would explain why zombies are such good hunters.

Dammit. Collin punches the ground in disgust. He ignored his symptoms all day, but really he knew something was wrong. Suddenly, Collin realizes Henry is at the top of the stairs. Shit! He's going to ruin the party.

*

Constance hates boys.

Her tactic worked. The two zombies immediately attacked Tom after she shot him in the leg. She ran to Bill's apartment to collect the kids, but they all hid after hearing the gunshots. By the time she gathered Brenda, Beth, and Bobbie together, the zombies were outside in the hall, soon joined by a badly mauled Tom-zombie.

After making sure the door was barricaded, Constance searched the entire apartment for weapons. Aside from a kitchen knife and a wooden baseball bat (and a surprising collection of porn mags), she came up empty. She's certain that Bill has another gun stashed somewhere in here, but it's hidden damn well.

"Connie, is this one of your dad's drills?" asks Beth, wiping tears from her eyes.

"It's Constance. And no, it's not a drill."

Bobbie starts bawling, and the zombies pound even harder on the front door. Constance kneels in front of Bobbie, holding his face in her hands.

"You have to stop crying. The zombies can smell your tears."

He looks at her wide-eyed, his face frozen with fear. He's terrified, but mercifully quiet, giving her some time to think.

"Can they break through the door?" asks Beth.

Constance shakes her head. "Not anytime soon."

"Can they break through the walls?"

"No," says Constance, a plan forming in her head. "But we can."

*

Henry stumbles down the hallway, looking drunker than KC has ever seen anyone. He's a mess, practically dead on his feet. Collin catches up to him at the end of the hall, drapes his coat over Henry's shoulders, and pushes him into the corner booth. Collin sits next to him, and Henry struggles vaguely.

KC rolls her eyes. Working at a strip club, she's seen a lifetime's worth of drunken male machismo bullshit. She looks away, waves over Pork Chop, now stationed behind the bar.

He's bleary-eyed and sweaty, a mad smile plastered over his face. "Get you a drink, pretty lady?"

"Please," she says. "Whatever's handy."

Pork Chop pours her a beer, plopping in some dye. He must have put in the wrong color, because the drink comes to her a funky orange. She shakes her head and sighs. The dumbass didn't even put it on her tab. Out of playful consideration for Collin's sense of detail, she grabs Collin's notepad.

He has drawn a little green heart around her name. There's an arrow through the heart, burning with a lovely green flame.

Sipping her drink, she thinks back over the past few weeks, reconsiders all of her interactions with Collin. She looks back at him. He's still sitting with Henry, though Henry is far more subdued, his forehead on the table. Seeing both men together is very revealing.

Henry taught KC how to survive, but maybe it's Collin who will show her how to truly live.

Night

The party is at the height of its revelry. Collin leans on the back of the bar, surveying his work. He imagines each of his friends as the center of individual green flame, each flame burning brightly and licking the ceiling.

Consuming.

Mr. John and Barbara are making out in the booth next to Henry's, probably on the verge of public sex. In an unexpected development, Bill and Charles are sitting at a booth in the far corner, kissing passionately. Charles' hand has been in Bill's lap for a long while. From all the way across the room, Henry hears Bill's zipper go down. Pork Chop is passed out. Marlene and Simon are giggling and laughing maniacally as they paint the mural, making the partygoers look like zombies. KC is in the bathroom.

The moans of at least a dozen zombies outside grow louder, and but no one seems to notice.

The zombies don't worry Collin. The front window is heavily reinforced, and the alley door to the basement is equally as solid. True, his friends will have to fight their way out in the morning, but they're more than capable. By then Collin will be dead, or undead, but he's determined to give them one great party before passing on.

KC returns from the bathroom, pausing for a moment to look at Henry. He looks stupidly back at her. What KC doesn't realize is that when Collin had shoved Henry into the booth, he'd used rope from the basement to secure Henry to the bench seat. At the time that had kept Henry subdued, but since Mr. John and Barbara sat nearby, he's fought sluggishly against his bonds. Henry can't see them over the high-backed booths, but he can definitely hear them.

Collin's heart trembles. Please don't let KC try to talk to Henry.

Thankfully, she returns to the bar.

"Henry's really drunk," she says, returning to her stool. "I mean really."

Collin nods. "He was pretty upset earlier."

"What were you two talking about?"

Collin considers. His hand throbs, and he imagines the zombie disease slowly working its way through his polluted bloodstream. It's only a matter of time.

"We were talking about you."

"Does he still love me?"

"I don't know if love is exactly the right word. It's fair to say that he hungers for you."

"What about you?"

Collin shrugs. "I don't think he cares one way or the other about me."

KC stands up, leaning over the bar. "No, jackass. I mean, how do you feel about me?"

Collin freezes. This is his moment.

But then he feels a slight vibration beneath his feet, and hears a loud crash outside.

What now?

He mumbles something to KC about having to check on the piss buckets, and dashes down to the basement, which is unusually drafty. Darting his flashlight beam across the room, he sees that one of the street entrance doors has been knocked completely off its hinges. Probably attracted by the light, a zombie stumbles down the stairs. Then another. Collin hears children yelling in the alley, footsteps running away.

What the hell?

*

Constance hates zombies.

More than boys and parents, she really hates zombies.

It took some doing, but Constance was able to cut through the drywall and plaster separating Bill's apartment from 5B. While she was working, the kids kept the zombies distracted at the front door.

When she finally gets the hole big enough, she runs to the front door, now barely hanging from its hinges. She grabs the kids and marches them back by lantern to the bedroom. There, she ushers them one-by-one through the whole in the closet wall, into the neighboring apartment, and to the window leading to the fire escape.

"Don't look at the blood," she says.

Once on the fire escape, she's immediately surprised by how loud the music is from below. What the hell are they thinking? Stupid, irresponsible adults.

It's awkward going by lantern light, so it takes her awhile to get all three kids down each flight of stairs. When they get to the second floor terrace, Beth tosses down the rope ladder, but Constance stops her before she can climb down.

Something's down there. Something moving.

Constance holds the lantern over the edge, illuminating at least a dozen undead faces. She tries pulling the ladder back up, but the zombies have already grabbed it and are trying to climb upward.

Shit!

"Back upstairs!" she shouts. If they can get to Dad's apartment on the seventh floor, she will have access to more ammunition.

They make it to the fourth floor platform, and then see that Tom, Arthur, and the other teenage zombie are on the platform above them. Constance rolls her eyes. Below, the fire escape rattles as the zombies fight their way upward.

They're trapped.

All too quickly, the fire escape lurches under the extra weight. Bolts pop from away from the brick, and the fire escape collapses.

*

"I know that this isn't the best time," says KC, sitting across from Henry. "But we need to talk."

Henry stares stupidly back at her, a line of drool spilling from his lip.

KC rolls her eyes. "This is dumb. You probably won't even remember this conversation tomorrow. Screw it. Just as well. This'll be like a dress rehearsal."

Henry moans at her. Never was much for conversation.

"Here's the thing, Henry. I think I love Collin. Now, I know that this may seem awkward, but I don't think there's any reason why we can't all live in the same building and co-exist. I mean, Bill and Barbara have been split up, and they're co-existing fine."

Behind KC, Barbara gasps in orgasmic pleasure. From across the room, Bill answers with his own moan of ecstasy.

"I just... I hope that we can be friends."

She reaches forward to pat Henry's cheek, and he snaps at her. She jerks her hand away.

"Fine, Henry. Have it your way. Real mature."

At that moment, Collin comes back down the hall, sees her with Henry, and pulls her out of the booth. Typical jealous male.

"Easy, Collin."

"Sorry," he says, pulling her gently behind the bar. Out of the corner of her eye, KC notices that the basement door is wide open. Ugh. She hopes that doesn't let the stink upstairs.

Collin sits on the floor behind the bar, motions for her to do the same. He looks about as drunk as KC feels.

Sitting on the floor, she puts a hand to Collin's face, so very cold. "I was just telling Henry that it's over between us. And that I'm moving on."

"Moving on?"

"I told him that I want to be with you."

Collin smiles wearily. "That's... that's great."

He pulls her close, burying his face against her neck. From across the bar, the noises get louder, more urgent. Heavy footsteps plod across the floor. Moans turn to gasps. Gasps turn to screams. It sounds like a full-blown orgy.

Eh, what's the harm? It is St. Patrick's Day, after all.

She puts her hand in Collin's lap, unzips his jeans. He kisses and licks at her neck. Even his tongue is cool. As she reaches into pants, he whispers haltingly to her.

"KC... do... you love... me?"

"I think so," she says.

He tries to say something else, but it comes out as a moan. She grabs ahold of his penis, which is entirely limp. Not surprising, since he's been drinking all day. He moans again.

"It's okay," she says. "It happens to a lot of guys. Just try to relax."

Collin squirms against her, still kissing at her neck. Licking. Biting.

Consuming.

All of the Above

To properly support the head and neck, an effective pillow maintains a height of approximately five inches.

This is the first thought to go through Larry's alcohol-scorched mind on Saturday morning, and he has no idea where the thought came from. It's true, of course, and his pillow is anything but effective, proper, or supportive. In fact, right now his pillow is a running shoe.

He sits up and stares at his shoe. Rubs his aching neck.

Slowly, he realizes that someone is watching him. It's his nine-year-old son Patrick, whose attention is torn between what's on t.v. – Spider-Man beating up a giant lizard – and what's on the family room floor – Larry.

"Hey, buddy," Larry says. "Daddy was just camping out on the floor. Practicing for, uh, camping."

"Are we going camping?"

"Um. Eventually?"

"What about snakes? I'm afraid of snakes."

"There are only about 8,000 venomous snakebites in this entire country, buddy, and no more than a dozen fatalities annually. That's .0025 of a percent of the population." The stats and calculations tumble over Larry's tongue, and again he has no idea where the facts come from.

Patrick cocks his head toward his father, though his gaze is fixated on the television. "That doesn't help, Dad."

Using all of his available stamina and coordination, Larry walks into the kitchen, sits down at the breakfast table, and closes his eyes. The darkness there, normally comforting, is tainted by the unpleasant sensation that starved maggots are gnawing at the backs of his eyelids. Larry opens his eyes, his groggy vision settling on the already open morning paper.

Larry's wife, Gail, stands over the stove tending to a pan of scrambled eggs. Not looking at him. "What time did you get home last night?"

Larry closes his eyes, preferring at least for the moment to face the hungry maggots. "Why ask when you know already?"

"Because I want to see if you were too drunk to know."

"Fine. It was three o'clock." She stares at him blankly. "Four o'clock." More staring. "Half past four?"

Gail turns back to the stove, stirs the eggs. "How much did you have to drink?"

"More than enough."

"What if you'd gotten into an accident? What if you'd killed yourself, or someone else?"

Gail audibly grits her teeth, and he cringes. Not because he has a problem with teeth-gritting, but because Gail looks like her mother when she grits.

"You shouldn't put milk in with the eggs," Larry says. "It makes them burn. Use a bit of water instead."

She stares at him, while the eggs behind her smolder. "What? You're the cook now?"

"Sorry. I guess I must have read that somewhere." But did he? No. He has no idea where he picked up this random bit of cooking knowledge. He turns the page of the newspaper, hoping for an interesting article to change the subject. Instead, he finds a report about the renovation of a local building, which contains a fact – that the building was built in 1934 – that he somehow knows to be untrue.

What. The. Hell?

On the back page, he finds the crossword. Gail had entered three of the answers before giving up. He picks up a pen and stares at the blank little squares on the page. A five-letter word for trout basket. Creel. A six-letter expression of annoyance. Tsk-tsk. A seven-letter word that makes animals' eyes shine in the dark.

"Tapetum?" he says.

"What?" Gail says, dumping the eggs into the wastebasket.

"Tapetum. It's what makes animals eyes glow."

"Uh-huh."

A five-letter word for a dispatch boat. A ten-letter breed of dog. An eleven-letter Latin illogical conclusion. Aviso. Rottweiler. Non sequitur.

On and on it goes until Larry finishes the entire puzzle. He moves on to yesterday's crossword, filling in the answers while Gail whips up a new batch of eggs.

"Whoa, check out the brain on Dad," Patrick says, standing behind Larry.

"Not bad, huh, kiddo?"

Patrick sits next to Larry, and Gail places a fresh plate of eggs in front of their son. She leans over Larry, mouthing the answers to the crossword.

"How did you know all of this?" she says.

Larry shrugs. "I just did."

Patrick puts down his fork. "Mom, these are the best eggs ever."

"Thanks," she says, sighing. "I used water instead of milk."

*

Later that morning, Gail stands over her husband. He's sprawled on the couch, drinking a concoction that smells like rotten juice. Patrick sits in the recliner. Tension has rooted into her lower back, like those damn vines with the spade-shaped leaves that plague her garden.

She clears her throat. "We'll need to drive separately to Mom's. I'm bringing over that table from the garage."

"That's today, isn't it?" Larry rubs the bridge of his nose.

"I figured Patrick and I'd go over early to spend some time with her. So you can wait until closer to dinner."

"Can I go later with dad?" Patrick says.

"No, that's okay," Larry says. "I'll just leave at the same time."

Her back tightens. Larry must know that he'll have a bad time at Mom's, but he goes anyway, out of some retarded sense of duty to Gail. Yet he'll spend the whole afternoon fidgeting and pouting and sighing like a baby.

She wrinkles her nose. "What are you drinking?"

He holds up the glass. "Pickle juice. Orange juice. Gatorade. Tomato juice. Hot sauce. Coffee."

She asks the only reasonable question. "Why?"

"To cure my..." His eyes flick to Patrick, now flipping through the channels. "My cold. I've got a whopper of a headache."

Patrick looks over. "I'm guessing all that drinking didn't help your cold, Dad."

Great. Gail picks up the drink and sniffs. It smells like something that would leak out of a casket. "And where did you get the idea for this unholy concoction?"

"It just occurred to me." He sits up quickly and points at the t.v. "Buddy, leave it here a second."

"*Fill in the Blank?*" Patrick says.

"Just for a minute."

"Okay, contestants," says the well-manicured host on the t.v. screen. "Welcome back to *Fill in the Blank*. It's time for the Final Blanks. Whoever gets the most correct answers, wins the round. Are you ready?"

The contestants nod.

"Blank predicted that Jesus was going to be born in Bethlehem."

"Micah," Larry says, before any of the contestants.

"Correct," the host says.

"BLANK contains all five vowels in reverse alphabetical order."

"Subcontinental and Unoriental," Larry says.

A second later, a female contestant says, "Subcontinental."

"Correct. We also would have accepted 'unoriental.'"

Patrick looks up at his dad, eyes and mouth wide open. Larry glances down at his son and smiles nervously. Gail just shakes her head. Something's up. Larry isn't a stupid man. He's remarkably clever, in fact, but he's never been good with facts. She can easily trounce him in Trivial Pursuit or Scrabble.

The host smiles. "In the nation of BLANK, the Indus River flows into the ocean."

"Pakistan." Larry turns to Gail. "How the hell did I know that? I couldn't even tell you where Pakistan is on a map." Larry closes his eyes. "Oh, wait. Yeah, I guess I can."

Gail shakes her head. She can't let this distract her from the topic at hand, not when she still has an ace in the hole.

"Instead of going to Mom's early," she says, "you could always finish painting the garage."

Larry shakes his head. "It's going to rain."

"If you don't want to do it, just say so. Have you been outside today? There isn't a cloud in the sky."

"It's going to rain. I'm sure of it."

"The paper said it'd be clear all weekend."

"The paper's wrong. Believe me. I read the whole thing, and I spotted several other bits of misinformation."

"Yeah. I bet you did."

*

Later, Larry migrates to the recliner and watches a historical documentary about the Civil War. A famous actor – maybe Morgan Freeman – was going on about how the war was the bloodiest fought in American history.

Larry shakes his head. "Well, they got that part all wrong."

"We're leaving," Gail says. "I'll see you over there."

"Do you need help with the table?" Larry spills himself out of the recliner.

"That's okay," Gail says, though her tone indicates that it clearly is not. She slams the side door just loud enough to rattle the windows.

Larry grunts. "God. Damn. It."

He stomps to the bedroom and jerks himself out of his pajamas. As he slides into his jeans, he marvels at the fact that one bale of cotton can produce a whopping 215 pairs of jeans. The official birthday of blue jeans is May 20th, also the date in 1570 that cartographer Abraham Ortelius created the first modern-day atlas. The dye used most commonly for jeans is phthalocyanine, an intensely colored macrocyclic compound with low solubility in virtually all solvents. As potential cancer-fighting properties of phthalocyanine cells flitter across Larry's consciousness, he clenches his teeth and growls. Takes a deep breath.

On his way out the door, he actually finds his car keys right where he expects them to be – an event that hasn't happened in years.

His Camry zips along the side streets of their neighborhood. Gail will take the highway, but the back roads will be faster. Veering the car onto County Road 19, he pulls out his cell phone and dials his friend Todd Leone.

Todd answers, his voice raw. "Why, man? Why so early?"

"Todd, did you know that your Italian surname is derived from the Latin *leonis*, a nickname for a fierce or brave warrior? Did you know that you share said surname with a Canadian businessman and criminal, an Italian long-distance runner, a food critic, a Canadian model, and a film director? Did you know all that, Todd? Because I sure as hell do. What the hell happened last night? I can't remember anything after the nacho dip."

"Hold on, Wiki-Larry. What the hell, man? I just woke up."

"Just tell me what we did last night."

"I dunno. Got pretty crazy. We mixed a bunch of crazy new drinks with shit Kevin found in his freezer. We played online video games with strangers. We had a Dorito-eating contest sometime after midnight. Oh, and we microwaved Scott's broken iPhone. That shit was hilarious."

"Uh-huh. Anything else?"

"Think that about covers it."

Larry sighs. "Thanks, Todd. I'll catch you later. Hey, don't forget that the *Beverly Hills 90210* marathon starts at five o'clock."

"Thanks." After a pause, Todd almost whispers, "Hey, how did you know that I watch *90210*?"

Larry clicks off. His car speeds past stretches of leafy trees and acres of cornfields. The long stalks blur together as Larry picks up speed. Each ear of corn has about 795 kernels in 16 rows. Wonderful to know.

Usually not one for excessive speed, today Larry knows exactly how fast he can accelerate into a turn without skidding off the road. As he zips around a bend at a swift seventy-two miles an hour, his head flashes with approximations of entry, apex, exit, weight, velocity, friction, braking point, and wind resistance.

Fat globs of rain strike the windshield, and he alters all his equations.

*

When Gail pulls their squat CRV into her mother's rain-splattered driveway, her mouth fall open and morphs into a smile. Larry's Camry already sits next to the garage. Larry's still behind the wheel. She wonders how long he's waited there and why. Because he wants to see her face when she sees that he beat her there? Or because he hates being alone with his mother-in-law? Or because he wants to gloat about the rain? She assumes all of the above.

Larry steps out of the car carrying an umbrella in one hand and waving with the other.

"Dad, how did you get here so fast?" Patrick says.

"I took the back roads," he says.

"You?" Gail steps into the misty rain and waves away his offer of an umbrella. "You get lost going through the drive-thru. You never take the back roads."

"Well, today I did. I knew the way, and I knew it'd be faster." Larry pauses. "And I wanted to help you with the table."

She speaks through a grin that she can't hold back. "Thanks."

Mom's house, where Gail grew up, is the largest home in one of the older suburbs around town, a neighborhood built when it first became fashionable for the wealthy to live outside of the downtown area. It also boasts the most immaculate garden on the street.

"Hi, Mom," Gail yells, as she and Larry maneuver the table into the house. Patrick holds open the front door.

"Careful with that," her mom, Samia Belanger, snaps. Her blond hair is pulled up into a tidy bun. Heavy makeup covers her beautiful face like acrylic paint. "You didn't use a blanket to move it? I hope it's not scuffed."

With that, Mom turns on her heel and returns to the kitchen. Larry and Gail exchange glances. Gail's struck by a gleam in his eye – something she hasn't seen since... Ever?

"Smells good, Mom," Larry says, following her into the kitchen.

Gail notices her mother cringe at the sound of Larry using the word "Mom" at her. She stands over the stove and stirs a pot of vegetable soup.

"Thank you, Lawrence," she says.

The kitchen is spotless. Even the presumably dirty coffee cup in the sink gleams.

Gail sits down at the kitchen table. "The garden looks great." It will win neighborhood pride awards – yet again.

"Patrick," Samia says, "why don't you go out to the garden and get some carrots for the salad?"

"Sure, Grandma."

Gail grabs a piece of celery from the fridge and fills a glass of water from the tap. She pulls the ice tray out of the freezer and slams it hard on the counter. A few blocks of ice leap out of the tray, as if startled. She drops them into her glass.

Samia watches as Gail munches on the celery. "Are you still *trying* to lose weight, Gail?"

"I'd like to lose a few more pounds."

"You know that's just an old wives tale," Samia says, refilling the ice tray and sliding it back in the freezer. "Drinking ice water doesn't really burn calories."

"Actually, that's not true." Larry holds up the water. "If you drink a sixteen-ounce glass of ice water, your system has to raise the temperature of the water from zero to thirty-seven degrees. To do that, you probably burn about seventeen calories. Now, that might now sound like much, but multiple that by the eight glasses of water that Gail likely drinks per day, and it could be as much as 136 calories. That's about what she'd burn walking for a half hour a day. It's just shy of a thousand calories a week."

"Thank you, Lawrence. You're insight is appreciated." Samia looks back at Gail. "That was the great thing about your father. He knew when to keep his mouth shut."

"Ben was a great guy," Larry says, "but he spent his whole life terrified of you. No matter what he did, it was never good enough. Right up until he had his stroke, he was just trying to do the impossible: to make you happy. And Gail has fallen into the same trap. She will always be too fat or too thin. Patrick will never be smart enough or well-mannered enough. And I'm never going to measure up to the husband that you sent to the grave."

A sickly sensation snuggles against Gail's spine. Her jaw clenches. She's mortified, though every word Larry says is true.

Still at the fridge, her mother grits her teeth, which is even more mortifying because Gail knows she does the exact same thing. Gail finishes her water and stomps out of the kitchen on shaky legs.

*

"These carrots are huge!" Patrick says, walking into the kitchen with an armful of carrots, the first vegetable to be canned commercially. Native to Afghanistan, this biennial plant features a flowering stem whose flowers produce a mericarp, a type of dry fruit.

Larry smiles at his son, who naturally remains oblivious to the avalanche of silence that threatens to smother Larry and Samia.

He takes Patrick's arrival as a cue to leave. "Pat, help your grandma with the carrots."

Walking briskly out of the kitchen, he finds Gail in the upstairs bathroom. He doesn't bother trying the knob. He knows it's locked.

Instead, he knocks three times on the door. "Can I come in, babe?"

The doorknob clicks. He enters.

Gail stands at the sink, gazing at her reflection in the spotless mirror.

"I'm sorry," he says. "I shouldn't have said that."

"It was all true."

"Well, that doesn't mean it needed said. I'm sorry. I've been Mr. Know-It-All all day, and it kind of went to my head. I've been kind of arrogant."

She smirks. "Kind of?"

He steps behind her, wraps his arms around her waist, and hugs her tight. They stare at themselves in the mirror. They've been married for over a dozen years. They've eaten countless meals together (7,817, actually), rode hundreds of thousands of miles, watched weeks worth of television, and shared thousands of kisses – all together. The weight of these statistics blurs his vision. He squeezes his eyes shut and refocuses on her reflection.

He sees her – the truth of her, not the image of her that's been carved and finished inside his head.

"You're beautiful," he says.

"Thank you."

"I'm sorry about staying out so late."

She pats his hand. "You can stay out all night and I wouldn't care. I just don't want you driving in that condition. Think about Patrick."

"It was stupid. I'm sorry."

"So, were there any hot girls at the bar last night?" She rocks gently back and forth, so that her backside rubs against his crotch.

"None as hot as you." Somehow, this is both true and not true.

He kisses her lightly on the back of the neck. She cocks her head so that he can kiss her behind the ear – her favorite spot. He squeezes her waist and continues kissing. She cranes her neck to kiss his lips.

After three minutes and thirty seconds of kissing, in which they each burn 91 calories, use all 34 facial muscles, and swap 57 million colonies of bacteria, Larry drops his hand into the waistband of her skirt.

"Larry, this isn't…" She gasps. "Don't…" She moans. "Don't…"

Larry's never been very good with his hands, but today is different. So different.

She lifts her skirt. "Don't stop kissing my neck."

*

Gail slips into the edges of dreamscape – a rain-spotted canvas of undulating bushes and quivering flowers – but the tremors inside her body snap her back to consciousness. She wakes with a wee gasp.

"You were snoring," Larry says, now sprawled out on the bathroom mat with Gail's upper body draped across his chest.

"Dammit. We didn't use any protection."

Larry pats her back. Those hands. Oh. My. God. Those hands. "You ovulated nine days ago, hon. No worries."

Gail does some math in her head and smiles. "What's gotten into you today? How are you suddenly so different?"

"I don't know. I just know all these things that I didn't know before. Like how to find Pakistan. Or your g-spot. I think… I think I know everything. I mean, not at once. But all day long, every piece of information I need, every question I have… it all just comes to me."

"Whatever." Gail bites his hairy chest. He tastes like salt and coffee.

Larry laughs. "I'm not kidding. Try me. Ask me anything."

"Okay, what is the name of Jupiter's largest moon?"
"Ganymede. But you wouldn't have known if that was right or wrong."

She elbows him, sits up, and grabs one of her mother's deodorants from under the sink. Her mother has three of everything in stock under there – toothpaste, deodorant, facial cleanser, and so on.

"Gail, no." Larry holds up a hand. "I don't want you smelling like your mother."

She shakes her head. "Okay, smarty-pants, tell me the ingredients in this."

"Active or inactive?"

"Inactive."

"Cyclopentasiloxane, stearyl alcohol, cyclohexasiloxane, PPG-14 butyl ether, phenyl-"

"Okay, enough." Her eyes widen. What if something's wrong with Larry's brain – like a tumor? "How the hell did you do that?"

Larry shrugs. "It just came to me."

"No, I mean how the hell did you know how to pronounce cyclo…" She squints closer at the list of ingredients. "Cyclopenta…"

"Cyclopentasiloxane," Larry finishes. "It's an odorless, silicone fluid also known as cyclic pentamer. Melts at negative 44 degrees Celsius. Boils at 90 degrees." He grabs the deodorant, runs his finger down the small print. "I know the same information for all of these. Plus a couple ingredients that conveniently weren't listed here. Huh."

"You're starting to creep me out." Gail pulls her panties on. "We should go back out there. God knows what my mom must think."

"That we had hot, wild sex in her bathroom?"

"Exactly." She smacks Larry's thigh. "Let's go."

They rise and wiggle into their respective clothing. Gail considers the day's events and watches her husband put on his shoes.

She rests her hand on his shoulder. "Okay, here's a question. What's the meaning of life?"

He opens his mouth, as if to speak, but closes it again. He stares upward, as if the answer hides beneath his eyelids or at the fringe of his frontal lobe. "An organismic state identified with growth, reproduction, metabolism, and reaction to stimuli?" Larry shakes his head. "No, that's not what you mean, is it? I... I don't know."

"Ha," Gail says. "Guess you don't know everything after all."

*

After an awkward but delicious dinner, Larry walks his family to the CRV and buckles Patrick securely. Gail kisses him on the back of the neck, her lips as light as thin layers of hardened protein called chitin covered with thousands of miniature scales and hairs called setae. In other words, as light as butterfly wings.

"Hey." She smacks his butt. "Take those back roads and show me how you got here so fast, okay?"

"Okay."

He climbs into his Camry and backs out of the driveway. Gail's question tickles his brain. What's the meaning of life? Butterfly wings. Tapetum. An atlas. Melting point. Snake venom. Water and eggs. Subcontinental. Ice melting in a belly. Dried fruit.

He shakes his head. It's all connected somehow.

Several miles later, his Camry speeds down Country Road 19. Stalks of corn flicker past, now wet with rain and glistening like jewels in the bright sun.

"If I know everything," he says aloud, "yet I don't know the meaning of life, then it follows that life has no meaning."

Larry pauses, taking in the full weight of this insight.

"Bummer."

He checks the rearview mirror to make sure Gail still follows behind. She is. His eyes flick back to the road.

Three quarters of a mile ahead, a red pickup truck comes from the opposite direction. All last night and into this morning, the driver of the truck played an online role-playing game, slaying hundreds of ogres and orcs.

Larry knows this.

A half mile. The man's nodding off, snug in a ray of sunshine.

Larry knows this.

A quarter mile. On its present course, the truck will drift over the yellow lane and run into Gail's CRV. It's all physics, probability, and geometry – a seamless calculation of velocity, momentum, impact, weight, and measure. The truck will kill his family.

Larry knows this.

A hundred yards. He beeps his horn. The old and rusted Ford – its gnarled grill the final resting place for hundreds of bugs – keeps on coming. Its driver-side tires inch toward the worn yellow line. The driver's head nods downward.

Larry cuts hard to the left.

His Camry hits the truck almost dead on. The impact sends his car tumbling across the road and through a buckshot-riddled speed limit sign. His air bag explodes outward. Dust fills the air – cornstarch used to lubricate the airbag during deployment. The rusty metal of the sign tears through the car. It punctures the air bag and slices into Larry's gut.

The car finally comes to a rest sideways in a ditch on the opposite side of the road. Larry hangs downward by his seatbelt, which in this case means he's dangling toward the passenger side of the car. He watches his small intestine, twenty feet long, spill out of his body and onto the passenger's seat and door.

Duodenum. Jejunum. Ileum. Epithelial tissue. Mucosa. Plicae circulares. It takes about eight hours for food to pass through the stomach and small intestine. By a coincidence Larry is only beginning to understand, that's about how long he's been awake today.

He tries calling for Gail, and that one syllable sprays chunky blood into the dusty air.

*

"Stay here," she tells Patrick. "Close your eyes."

She slams the door before her son can respond and runs toward Larry's Camry now lying sideways in the ditch. The driver of the truck lies in the road directly in her path – and at the end of a trail of blood and gore. His arm looks like it has an extra elbow. Shredded skin covers his arms and face. He screams at her for help, his jaw hanging crooked like a door half off its hinges.

Her shadow falls over him. She pulls out her phone. No signal. She opens her wallet, though she's not sure why. "I'm... I'm sorry." She drops her driver's license next to the man. "I have to go."

Even from several steps away, she hears Larry's ragged breathing, like someone sucking air through a damp sponge. When she reaches the ditch, she vomits bits of soup and salad into the wet grass. She wipes bits of carrot from her mouth and holds onto the Camry. The ditch is deep enough that she's able to bend over the edge of the car and reach into Larry's broken driver's side window. Her husband stares up at her. Her heart squirms into her belly. Oh, God. So much blood.

He reaches for her.

"Larry." She grabs his bloody hand. "I'm here. I'm right here."

He stares at her with remarkably focused eyes. "Patrick?"

"He's okay." She squeezes his hand. "What happened, Larry? Was there an animal in the road? Did a tire blow? Did you lose control?"

"The answer is..." He closes his eyes and smiles. His grip tightens. He coughs and takes his last breath. "It's all of the above."

Larry's hand goes limp, but she keeps squeezing. White dust and blood cover her husband's face. Back in the road, the other man finally stops screaming. She needs to remember to get her license back. She needs to go to Patrick. She needs to tell him his father's last words. She's scared to death she might forget.

The Hole in Me

The first time Conway Morris saw a demon, he spent the rest of the day hiding in his office waiting for his khakis to dry. The demon's name was Chad.

After meeting the demon, he sat for hours behind his desk. Naked from the waist down, his thighs kissed hard against the leather chair. He kept the lights low, and shadows festered around the well-used couch, the chairs in front of his desk, and the credenza. Instead of artwork, the walls featured promotional Way-Mor posters for his business – blown-up pictures of adults eating food, playing games, and drinking booze.

He hadn't felt such crippling loneliness in years. The emptiness pressed down on him like a hole from which he could not escape. Around nine o'clock that evening, someone knocked on his door.

Knock knock.

It sounded like shovelfuls of dirt tossed on a coffin.

"Go away," he said.

Trasci stepped inside anyway and flicked on a light. The top three buttons of her wrinkled Way-Mor uniform shirt were unbuttoned.

"June said you've been in here most of the night," she said. The young woman was oblivious to the translucent pair of feathery wings stretching upward from her shoulders and almost scraping the ceiling.

Most days, Conway barely noticed the wings anymore.

"I've had a lot of paperwork to do," he said.

She leaned over the desk. Her straight black hair was pulled up, but a few stray bangs spilled forward. Her nametag read TRACY because she had gotten tired of customers mispronouncing the real spelling. *Tras-key. Trays-key. Truss-ki.*

"Yeah," she said, placing a nail mostly covered with purple nail polish upon the blank page that had been daring him to write.

"Looks like you're making a lot of progress here."

"Trase, I'm not in the mood tonight."

"Well, you better get in the mood, Connie." She batted her eyelashes. "Because your nine o'clock is here."

"My what?" He slapped a hand to his face. "Oh, shit."

A new gal was interviewing for his special events coordinator position. His damp pants and underwear hung from his hat rack on the wall, taunting him.

Trasci stared at him, and he couldn't hold her gaze. The loneliness bowed his head and bent his shoulders. Her wings didn't help but they should have.

"You feeling okay?" she said. "Something about you is off."

"I've got a headache is all." He pointed at his credenza. "Please hand me her file."

Trasci sauntered across the room, making a big show of bending over to retrieve the file, accidentally dropping it, and then bending over still further to pick it up again. Her engagement ring spat back the light from his desk lamp.

He rolled his eyes. "Trase, knock it off."

"What's napping up your butt tonight?"

In the hallway, heels clacked against tile.

Click clack.

It sounded like bone clacking against bone. This must be his nine o'clock. The heels tapped closer and closer. Would she be a demon, too? Dread soured in his belly. With each click and clack, he imagined sleepy fingers strolling down his spine, in search of shelter inside his exposed ass.

Click clack.

Between the shoulder blades.

Click clack.

Over the small of his back.

Click clack.

Past his waist.

A young blond peeked around the corner. Pink lipstick highlighted her confident smile. Her blue eyes locked onto his, through a pair of fashionable glasses that she probably didn't need to wear. The doorway obscured her wings.

"Can I come in, Mr. Morris?" she said.

"Uh," was all he could say.

"Call him Connie," Trasci said, tossing the folder onto his desk. "He likes it."

The young woman stepped inside, revealing a white pair of pillowy wings. Conway sighed and wiped a few drops of sweat from his brow. The nine o'clock wore a charcoal grey skirt suit. She approached his desk, hand outstretched.

"I'm Allison Grant," she said. "I'm so excited to meet you, Mr. Morris."

"Pardon me if I don't get up," he said, extending a hand. "I've got a terrible headache."

She met his hand with a vigorous group. Her lips twitched slightly at the feel of his damp palm. Damn it.

"I'm sorry," she said. "Should we reschedule?"

They should've, but he needed her here. Surely her angelic presence would lift him out of this hole.

He shook his head. "Onward. I'm fine."

She sat down, eyes never leaving his. He couldn't hold her gaze. Her wings twitched behind her as if ruffled by a breeze. What was disturbing them? It had to be the demon, Chad.

"You visited our management and organizational behavior class two years ago," she said. "I was so impressed with your story. You came from nothing. You had no family to help you, and no formal education. Yet, a few short years later, you built the Way-Mor empire."

"I'd hardly call it an empire." He waved away the compliment he should have accepted graciously.

"Fifteen locations in a dozen states," she said. "And two more on the way."

"You've done your homework."

"I'm excited to be a part of your team, Mr. Morris."

"Please. Call me Connie."

"Ever since you visited our class, I've wanted to work with you and learn your secret."

"My secret?" His head snapped upward, and he realized that he'd been slouching. He cleared his throat. "What secret?"

Her eye contact faltered. "I just meant, whatever made you so successful in such a short time."

"Ah. Well." He glanced down at her file, trying to make sense of her work experience, degrees, achievements, and ambitions.

Normally, he wouldn't bother glancing at a candidate's resume during an interview. Nor would he need a sheet of prescribed questions. "Uh. Yes. Um, why don't you tell me a little about yourself? No. Better. Why don't you tell me where you see yourself in five years?"

She bit back a frown. "Okay. I'd like to take on increasing responsibility…"

Her words swam past him, diving deeper into the moment that he could no longer sustain. Quickly, he found his attention hovering far above that moment. What the hell was going on here? Had he left all of his charm and poise in his pants?

Damn. The pants.

It had started as a normal day. He'd checked the reports of last night's business and had read a few emails. Before the dinner rush, he'd walked the floor with June, the general manager.

Video games chirped and flashed. Mirrors on the ceiling and walls expanded the depths of his domain, the windowless heaven known as Way-Mor. Hundreds of liquor bottles gleamed behind the bar. The tables in the dining room stood at attention, lined up like soldiers.

Angel wings stretched over everyone's heads, as translucent as tissue yet as thick as steak. They glowed a hundred shades of white, from that of a gleaming cloud on a sunny day to a sweat stained t-shirt ready to be turned into rags.

June walked ahead of him, her wings arched slightly back. She was explaining about a restaurant management application, showing him on her tablet how it would streamline all their compliance, training, store audits, and readiness reports.

"That's incredible," he said.

"No, I'm incredible," she said, "but you can show me that by giving me more vacation time."

He laughed and pretended to wave at an employee across the complex. In truth, he was just running his hand through her feathery goodness.

"Have you met Chad?" she said.

"What?" he said.

His office wrapped around his slouched form. A question hung in the air.

"What?" he said.

He was back with his interview, who now stared at him and

frowned. What was her name? Alice? He tried looking through her glasses into her eyes, but his gaze quickly jerked away, as if he'd held his fingertip to a burning flame. Alexis?

"Are you sure we shouldn't reschedule?" she said, rising to her feet. "I really don't want to—"

"No," he said, rising from his seat.

His ass skin ripped away from leather, a noise like duct tape being yanked from carpet. He yelped. Her eyes widened to match the circular shape of her glasses. Ali? She jumped backward, tumbling over her chair. Halley? He grabbed her resume, which revealed her name to be—

"Allison," he shouted. "Wait."

He came out from behind his desk, her resume pressed to his groin. His junk rubbed against her bulleted list of volunteer activities. She crawled away from him, almost to the door.

"Please," he said. "Don't go. I'll tell you my secret."

One of her trembling hands rested on the doorknob. Her other clutched her high heels. She looked back at him through crooked glasses.

"Your secret?"

He nodded, crushing her personal statement into his pubes.

"I see angels."

She rolled her eyes, fumbled out the door, and slammed it shut.

"Damn it." He balled up her resume and threw it after her.

At that moment, June opened the door.

"What the hell just—" June started.

The crumpled paper bounced off her forehead.

"Happened?" she finished. Her eyes settled on his groin. "Exposing yourself so soon, Connie? You usually wait until at least the second week of work."

He put his hands on his hips, offering her a view she'd seen more than once. "No more appointments today, June. You're in charge."

She sighed. "I'll contain my excitement."

Without another word, she turned around, offering him a brief eyeful of her toned ass and luxurious wings.

He'd followed that same view earlier toward the vestibule of Way-Mor's flagship location. She had led him through the main bar and past bare blue pool tables, each as serene as a kiddie pool. A familiar beat thumped over the speakers. He had stopped briefly at the bar to flirt with the bartender and grab a beer.

As usual, June talked while she walked. "You'll like Chad. He's our new greeter. He's from the independent living Village just down the road."

"That place for retards?"

"Mentally disabled, Connie. It'll be great PR for us. People love him already."

"He's not depressing, is he?" He high-fived one of the waitresses walking past and his hand lingered in the air to stroke June's wings. "Those wretches at the front of Wal-Mart always make me want to slit my damn throat."

"So, he shouldn't be wearing a blue vest, then?"

He ignored her smart-assery and glanced into a mirror. Reflections never showed wings, so he only stared at his reflection – not June's. He checked his posture, erect but relaxed, and rotated his neck. This was part of his ritual whenever meeting someone for the first time, which also included flexing his fingers to ensure a proper handshake and practicing his smile.

"Why are you smiling?" June said. "It's creepy."

"I'm loving life, Junebug. You should try it some time."

"My job necessitates that I have no life, Connie. But if you'd like to pay me more vacation time—"

Conway stepped past her into the atrium, a cavernous space containing a welcome center, a coat check, and tabletop video games. The Way-Mor mascot, a giant beaver, danced with some kids in the corner. The beaver waved to him, and he raised his glass of beer in salute. High on the wall, an oversized map of the Way-Mor facility proclaimed, *"You are here."*

He smiled at a gaggle of young businesspeople chatting near the front doors. They looked stressed and thirsty – perfect customers. Oddly, their wings twitched slightly, like bushes rooted beside a busy roadway.

Taking another sip of malty goodness, he stepped around the crowd in search of this Chad. A forest of angel wings parted. He almost dropped his beer.

Chad's blond hair looked like a used mop plopping upon his scalp. A cleft chin formed a butt-shape right under his stupid smile, which was framed by dried saliva.

A pair of bat-like wings grew upward out of the man's shoulders. Gnarly spindles of misshapen bone framed the horrid constructions. Bruised slices of flesh stretched between the boney protrusions. Conway almost threw up.

Instead, he pissed himself.

A knock at his office door pulled him out of his thoughts.

Knock knock.

It sounded like a heartbeat heard from the inside.

He sat Indian-style on the floor, his back against the front of his desk. The carpet kneaded at his bare ass. It'd been ages since Allison and June had left. Since then, he hadn't moved except to rub his temples, wipe his nose, and scratch his balls.

Trasci opened the door and stared at him. He didn't bother covering himself.

"Hey, Connie," she said. "I just wanted to see if—"

"You wanted to make sure I'm not on the verge of a complete breakdown. I'm fine. I'm fine."

"Actually, I just wondered if you wouldn't mind sharing some of whatever drugs you've been taking. Sounds like wild stuff, and my shift is crawling tonight."

"I'm not on anything," he said.

She closed the door behind her. Pulling out a crumpled pack of menthols, she grabbed his empty beer glass from the desk and sat beside him. She was close enough to grab his exposed penis. Not likely to happen, but a nice thought.

"You told the new girl you see angels?"

"New girl? Who said she's hired?"

"After that fiasco, you better hire her or you'll be dealing with a lawsuit."

She lit a cigarette and exhaled blue smoke into the air. Her lips pursed together into a kiss. The cloud whirled like a lazy orgy of ghosts.

"You only ever screwed me when it was cold outside," he said. "I think you just liked being able to smoke indoors."

She ashed in his beer glass. "Angels, Connie?"

He embraced her hand – the one with the cigarette – and pulled it toward his face. He kissed the back of her palm, turned her hand over, and took a drag. Glassy smoke swept into his lungs. His blood buzzed.

"Yeah, fucking angels, Trase." He shifted his weight a little, so the carpet would paw at his ass. "You know I came from nothing, right?"

"Uh-huh."

"Well, back then, I used to spend a lot of time in the library."

"What library?"

"Doesn't matter. One day, I found this damn self-help book. I read it cover-to-cover in one afternoon while sipping on cheap wine. I don't even remember the title or author. I've searched for it since, and I can't find the damn thing. But one chapter had an exercise. It said that if you want to empower yourself, to start visualizing angel wings growing out of everyone around you."

"Angel wings?"

"Yeah, like you have to see the good in people, that at their core we all want to help each other. It makes you connect with people. It empowers you. It lifts you up. At least, it did for me."

"So, you read a book in the library, started hallucinating angels, and started your own multi-million-dollar business? Well done."

He laughed. "Actually, I read a book, passed out drunk, woke up in a puddle of my own filth, and then started seeing angels. It came gradually at first. I could only visualize the wings a few seconds at a time. But I spent weeks working at it. I'd sit in the park for hours, visualizing wings and feathers."

"Didn't you have a job?"

"Doesn't matter."

"Were you homeless?"

"Doesn't matter."

"Didn't you have friends or family?"

"None of it matters." He shook his head. "All that matters is that before I saw you angels, I was in a hole filled with smothering emptiness. I was born alone. No matter what I did to try to dig out, I couldn't do it. I've never been able to handle people. Or life. Everything held me down in that hole.

"Now, I only ever see angel wings. I can't not see them. I'm successful and I've got all the sex and money I could need. I thought you angels pulled me out of the hole, because I hadn't felt that loneliness in so long. But today I realized that I'm still in that hole. I'm still alone. I just haven't been able to feel it. I've been numb to it because I've been surrounded by angels."

"So what happened today?"

"Chad happened. He's different."

"He doesn't have wings?"

"Not like yours, no." He reached up and stroked her wings.

"Oh, fuck me. You're touching them, aren't you?"

"Can you feel it?"

"Yes, Connie. I feel it. And it turns me on in all manner of not at all. Cut it out, man."

Her jerked his hand back. "Sorry."

She took a thoughtful drag and squinted at him. "Wait a second. Is that why we never did it missionary? Because of the wings?"

He nodded. "I hated the thought of crushing them."

She rubbed the bridge of her nose. "When we did it doggie style, I always had this sense you were doing something strange behind my back. The wings?"

"Stroking them. Yes."

"You're weirding me out, Connie. I really think you should talk to someone."

"That's what I'm doing right now."

"Someone qualified."

"You have a bachelor's degree, right?"

"Yes. In History. And I'm using it to wait tables. Hurray."

"You're very good at what you do."

"Okay." She wiped her palm through the air between them, as if clearing a chalkboard. "What's the deal with Chad's wings? You said they were different."

He nodded. "They're leathery nasty things. Like a bat. Or a demon."

"A demon, Connie?"

"Yeah. A demon. I got so scared, I fucking pissed my pants. I had to hide it by spilling a beer all over my crotch. I've been hiding in here since."

"From a demon?"

"Yeah. From a demon. And now I'm back in my hole."

"Can I do something to help?"

He stared through her wings at the ceiling. Putting that word out there – *demon* – made him realize what he needed to do.

"Help? Yeah, would you mind scrounging me up some pants?

I'll eventually need to go home. Until then, I'd like to lie down."

"Sure, Connie."

Except he didn't need to lie down. He didn't need to go home. He needed to get up and go out.

Later, he snuck out one of the rear employee doors wearing the bottom half of the damn beaver outfit and a pair of gloves from the stockroom. The heavy fur in the inner thighs shushed together. His beaver tail flapped against the back of his knees.

"You're hilarious, Trase," he said to himself. "Very funny."

He traipsed through several empty and abandoned lots before reaching the Village, a cluster of cottages surrounding a dimly lit park. At this hour, only a few exterior lights glowed on the grounds. All but one of the cottages sat dark. Conway squatted in a flowerbed next to the lit window. His beaver thighs itched and his tail scraped at the bark mulch.

Sure enough, the retarded demon sat at a square kitchen table staring at a checkerboard turned sideways. About half the pieces sat next to the board. Red had a slight advantage. Chad's ugly wings stretched high over the board, filtering the fluorescent light into something piss-colored. Chad frowned at the board, jumped a black checker over a red, and kinged himself. He shook his head and moved a red checker into the fray.

The damn demon was playing with himself.

The itch in Conway's beaver thighs rose from murmur to scream. He twisted around and scratched between his legs. Bark crunched beneath him. When he looked back in the window, Chad was staring right at him.

"Shit." Conway ducked behind a bush.

Several frantic heartbeats later, Chad's door opened. A distorted rectangle shone over the lawn. A man-shaped silhouette stepped into the lit frame.

"Mr. Morris, sir?" he said. "Are you here for my prohibition?"

Conway rose from the bushes. "Your what?"

"Ms. June said I'd have a prohibition period at work, to make sure I'm a part of the team. Are you here for my prohibition?"

"Probation. Yes, that's why I'm here."

"I like your furry pants."

"Thank you, Chad. Can I come in?"

A few footsteps later, he sat at the kitchen table across from the terrible demon. The room stank of old fruit. Chad's wings lurked in the air, swaying back and forth like a snake ready to lunge. He tried to stare Chad in the eye, but the young man's gaze probed back all the deeper, as if drilling inside Conway's skull.

"So, how was your first day?" Conway said.

Chad smiled. "I met a lot of new friends. They all laughed at my jokes."

"Oh, yeah?"

"Would you like to hear one?"

Conway fidgeted with his gloves. "Sure."

"Knock-knock."

"Who's there?"

"Ya."

"Ya who?"

Chad smiled with his perfect teeth. "Boy, you sure are excited to see me."

Conway forced himself to laugh.

"Knock-knock," Chad said.

"Who's there?"

"Avenue."

"Avenue who, Chad?"

"'Aven't you knocked on this door before?"

This time Conway roared. He slapped his gloved hand upon the table hard enough to jostle the checkers. Several kings lost their crowns. He reached out and placed a black checker on top of another.

"It's okay," Chad said. "It wasn't a very good game any way. It's no fun playing by yourself."

"I wonder if some of us are meant to be alone, Chad."

Conway tapped a checker on the table.

Tip tap.

It sounded like rain against hard soil, like chattering teeth heard through muscle and bone.

"Maybe fate gives us a gift, the ability to see things that no one else can, and the price of that gift is loneliness. And with that gift, we sometimes see things that we don't want to see – things that need destroyed."

Chad flashed his pearly teeth. "Did you bring me a gift?"

He shook his head. "No, but I've got a game we can play,

Chad. Just close your eyes."

Chad shut his eyes tight, scrunching his face like an overjoyed raisin. "I've never played this game before. What are the rules?"

"You can't move a muscle or open your eyes. No matter what I do, stay perfectly still."

Conway rose, and Chad's wings twitched in response. The ragged flaps of flesh clenched the air above Chad's head. The jagged bones topping each wing jabbed Conway's direction. He stepped behind the young man.

Chad smelled of processed cheese and chalk. His shoulders sagged and his demon wings flexed. Conway imagined strangling him from behind, but to do so, he'd have to reach through that scarred flesh. The goosepimpled skin hung taut and translucent, a torn page riddled with blemishes and scabs. The thought of touching the things, even with gloves, nearly crippled him.

Instead, he stepped to Chad's front. The laminate tile floor squelched beneath his beaver feet. Conway flexed his gloved hands in front of the boy's throat. Chad smiled and swayed, as if he had to pee. Conway counted backwards from five, grabbed the boy's thin neck, and squeezed.

Chad's smile wavered.

Conway squeezed.

A lot happened at once.

Checkers clattered on the sticky floor.

The stink of urine soaked the air.

Chad's wings flapped and stabbed at Conway.

Fresh pee dripped beneath the boy's seat.

Conway closed his eyes for a moment, unable to stare at either the boy's innocent smile or his wings' menacing motions. Eyes closed, he lost his balance, sidestepped, slid on a mess of checkers and piss, and pitched forward onto Chad.

Conway opened his eyes. The boy's horrid wings wiggled beneath Chad's back. The young retard stared up at him, no longer smiling. Conway's knees pinned down one of Chad's arms. His other arm reached up. Conway braced himself for an eye gouge or scratch.

Instead, Chad reached past his head. Conway stared at a black checker, focusing on that little hole, now so much smaller on the floor. Chad's hand moved in the periphery of his vision. The boy's face darkened, first red as a checker and then purple.

Something knocked against the floor, perhaps Chad's feet.
Knock knock.

Trembling, Conway blinked long and hard, shuffling visions of a dying disabled boy, throbbing shadows, a darkening face, a piercing light, a grave seen from inside, wings as lifeless as cold cuts, and a coffin door slamming shut.

Conway slept easy that night.

He woke even easier.

Days and nights passed.

He pondered all that he had seen and done. Things changed.

A few moments ago, he sat in the atrium at a Ms. Pac-Man table-top arcade game. The table featured a chair at either end, so that two players could compete. The game blipped its classic song. Ms. Pac-Man evaded four ghosts while munching dot after dot.

Nearby, his new special events coordinator Allison greeted a man in a suit. Their wings brushed together over their heads. She led him into the bowels of Way-Mor, expounding about the many amenities available for guests of all ages.

Trasci's voice spoke from over Conway's shoulder. "I should have known I'd find you here. Don't you have anything better to do?"

He turned to her. Her black hair was pulled back into a tidy ponytail. Her red nail polish matched her red dress shirt. Upon her breast, a crooked nametag read, "TRASCI – Assistant Manager."

Conway shook his head. "If you're doing your job, then no, I don't have anything better to do."

Trasci rolled her eyes. "I need a cigarette."

"So go have one."

She batted his words out of the air. "I've got too much to do."

"I bet you're counting the days until June gets back."

Her eyes pulsed. "Oh. She sent us a postcard."

She reached into her pants pocket and produced a postcard depicting a peaceful beach. June had written in big bold letters "I AM HERE" in the perfect sky and drawn on arrow from the words onto the beach.

"I love it," Conway said.

"The little shit didn't even bother writing any message." She flipped the card to reveal a mostly blank back, except for Way-Mor's address in care of Connie Morris.

"She said what she needed to."

"Whatever. Some of us have work to do." She tossed him the card and started to walk away. She stopped and clutched her tablet to her chest. "Do you still see wings, Connie?"

"I do."

"Are you still in your hole?"

He shook his head. "I think the hole is in me."

"I've been saying that for years."

"I've been scared all my life of dying alone, Trase. We're alone before we're born. We're alone after we die. To go away from one, is to go toward another. Pass through either door and you're on your own. It's what happens between those doors that matters."

She stared at him. "I need a cigarette."

Her heels clicked and clacked away, leaving Conway with his thoughts. He looked at the frozen beach and the floating ghosts and the front door and the canceled stamp and the stupid beaver and the map on the wall.

You are here.

For the first time in his life, Conway really is here.

Soon, Chad walks in, carrying his checkerboard. Conway smiles and waves. Chad takes the seat opposite him, his slouched back to the door. His gnarly wings loom overhead, cracked and leathery.

"Knock knock," Chad says.

"Who's there?"

"Justin." He bites back a grin.

"Justin who?"

"Just in the neighborhood. Thought I'd drop by."

Conway claps. "Good one, Chad. Are you ready to play?"

Chad's eyes pop open. He grips the table. "We're not playing prohibition again, are we?"

"No." Conway shakes his head. "Remember what I said. You don't ever have to play prohibition again. You should forget all about that night."

That night seems like a lifetime ago.

Conway had choked Chad to the verge of death. The boy's wings had stopped flapping. His face had bulged like a purple grape. But then Chad's feet had knocked on the floor.

Knock knock.

It sounded as final as birth, as liberating as death. Unable to face his victim, he closed his eyes. He saw his infant self waiting to be born and his decaying corpse patiently rotting. He saw his whole life in-between, desperate and clinging to something – to anything or anyone.

So he let go.

He fell backward and his beaver tail slapped the sticky floor. Chad gasped and sputtered. He rolled over, demon wings flapping sluggishly.

"You were touching my wings, weren't you?" Conway said. "You can see them."

Chad only coughed in response. "Did I win the game?"

"Yeah, Chad. You won."

Conway mopped up piss while Chad put away his checkers. He washed the boy's pants and underwear in the sink. Conway made the boy a glass of warm milk and walked back to the office.

And now, here they sit.

Conway studies the checkerboard, now eclipsing the pixelated ghosts below. He glances at Chad, who's either watching the flatscreen anchored to the wall or staring at Conway's wings.

He jumps one of Chad's black checkers.

"I'm sorry for this, Mr. Conway," Chad said.

"Call me Connie, damn it."

Chad triple-jumps his way to Conway's side of the board.

"Shit." Conway crowns the black checker.

"Now I can go forward and back," Chad reminds him.

Conway laughs. "You sure can, Chad. But I wonder if the answer isn't to go a completely different direction."

"I don't think the rules let you, Mr. Connie."

He smiles at the young man. "That's why you need the angels."

Chad bows his head toward the board and whispers, "Are there angels in this game?"

"No, buddy," Conway whispers back. "All the angels are here on earth." He slides his red checker from there to here.

It sounds like nothing at all.

Low Hanging Sun

The evening's darkness is fading in when the Faithful come to kill the man once known as Murphy. He's standing near the end of a long ticket line that stretches all the way from the New Theatre to the edges of Lunar Acres—the floating fortress that houses the last scraps of human civilization. He stares into the water, entranced by a glistening blood slick and pondering the precipice of past and present.

Their squishy footsteps register too late. When he pivots and throws up an elbow, a rusty blade dives into his shoulder. Sharp agony crackles inside the wound. He grunts and thrusts his palm into his hooded attacker's face. Its monstrous head snaps backward.

Dusk's greenish light shimmers on its scaly face. Goggles cover its eyes. He yanks the hose running from its nostrils to its neck gills. Greenish blue blood arcs through the air. He unsheathes his sword and uses his attacker as a shield. As he expected, at least two more charge forward. Metal clangs against metal.

His own hood falls backward, revealing his scarred right cheek and the long knotted braids of the beard covering the left half of his face.

"It's Halfbeard!" a boy yells.

Many in the assembled crowd applaud. A few try to start a chant, but like a stubborn flame chewing wet wood it doesn't take. The children watch his grisly work, eyes full of wonder. Their parents clutch leather bags filled with scales.

His palms and feet smolder angrily. He stabs and slices at his attackers. His sword gashes a Faithful's throat. It gurgles and hisses. His shoulder screams as he pivots and slashes another. He cracks the neck of the first attacker—now bleeding from multiple stab wounds—but doesn't let the body fall. Time to give the crowd what they want—and provide himself a distraction. He shifts behind his victim, a female. No matter. Her breasts make it easier to hold upright. He steadies his blade horizontal below its belly. The metal's ridged close to the guard, and he scrapes it upward.

Cool-colored scales pop off the bitch's belly, revealing pale flesh beneath. The scales clatter onto the wooden dock, and the crowd lunges forward cheering and cursing all at once. He scrapes two more times before letting the stripped corpse thud downward. Replacing his hood and sheathing his sword, he steps away from the swarming mob.

Sharp pain flares in his chest.

And then again.

He looks down.

Two thick harpoons now jut out of his pectoral muscles. Someone shot him from behind. The Faithful were a distraction for the real attack, a way of flushing him out.

"Motherfucker," he says, the words already seasoned with blood.

Three staggered steps later, he stumbles off the dock and splashes into the ocean. As he sinks below, he reads the painted banner spread over the boardwalk one last time. *Tonight: World Premier of the Legend of Halfbeard!*

Bubbles swarm around him. He flails at the water and fumbles at the spears protruding from his chest, making little progress with either. The putrid ocean drags him down.

*

More than a lifetime ago, Murphy woke with something slippery and thick wiggling in his gut. The air lay salty on his chalky tongue. He hadn't remembered drinking that much, and yet here he was on the couch and not his bed wearing only a torn bathrobe from which several tattoos peeked curiously out at this strange new day. He rose on unsteady legs, and the floor lurched beneath him. The bottoms of his feet ached as if he'd walked across hot asphalt. The hell?

He stagger-limped down the hall. His bedroom door—across from the bathroom—stood open. Last night's tips from the bar lay crumpled and scattered on the floor next to his dusty guitar case. The pockets of his jeans were turned inside-out as if the denim was shrugging "whatchagonnado." He shook his head. Those bills and coins should've been breeding in a bank instead of slipping through his fingers. He'd never been good with money. *You drink too much and save too little*, is what she'd said before leaving for the last time. Now here he was in California and she might as well have been a world away. That was years ago, and still her words haunted him.

Only one door in the hallway was shut, the one that he and his housemate Keith subleased to a guy they privately called the Shut-In. He vaguely remembered being surprised to find the door open when he'd come home last night.

Wincing, he shuffled into the bathroom and tried to focus on the morning ritual ahead—watching *The Daily Show*, eating a bowl of Special K, and reading yesterday's writing. He felt close on this current screenplay. This could be the one to finally pay off—the one to make him rich and famous and earn him a house right on the ocean. All he really wanted was to see one of his stories on the big screen. The money wouldn't hurt, either. A beachfront house. He wanted to wake up with the ocean at this door.

The floor swayed again. He gripped the wall. Dull pain sizzled in his palm.

"Motherfucker," he said, surprised at the grit in his voice.

He turned his palm over. His jaw dropped open. His heartbeat took up a jagged punk rhythm. The tender flesh of both his palms swelled upward as if he'd gotten a new tattoo, except there was no ink—only heat and soreness. He tilted both hands and caught maybe a slight glimpse of a simple yet foreign symbol. A stylized X or a distorted star. Leaning against the wall, he checked the bottoms of his feet. They, too, had the same mysterious tenderness and raised flesh. His stomach groaned. The hell?

He limped to the toilet and pissed, gripping only with his fingertips in case the affliction was contagious. After flushing, he went to the mirror, fearful that he might see raised flesh on his face. Thankfully, only a few days of stubble marred his features.

Whatever had happened to his hands and feet, it probably needed cleaned. He turned on the shower. The water smelled a bit salty and wasn't at all hot, but it'd have to do. He climbed inside and washed yesterday off of him, leaning all the while against the tile. His vertigo wasn't improving but last night's memories were coming back.

He'd come home relatively sober and the Shut-In greeted him with an ornate glass bottle—no label. The Shut-In had insisted he drink each shot the same way, bending over the table and grasping the wooden shot glass between his teeth—hands outstretched—then leaping upward so that his feet left the ground. In mid-air, the liquor barreled down his throat. He'd ended the shot upright, arms stretched to the sky, and spit out the wooden glass.

"Ahoy," he'd said, per The Shut-In's instructions.

He remembered many such shots, and his mysterious sub-leaser ranting about rising tides and global reckonings and buried treasures and ill-fated awakenings.

"Ahoy," he said now. "Dammit."

Leaning on the tile, he squirted a dollop of shaving cream onto the back of his hand and spread it onto his checks and neck. He scraped a vertical stripe down his right cheek. Several scrapes later, the house lurched sideways.

He almost fell except he grabbed the shower curtain rod, which broke free from the wall and he fell anyway, tangled in the shower curtain. The floor smacked his shoulder.

"The hell?" he said.

He figured it to be an earthquake although the motion felt too protracted and smooth. Floorboards creaked a whale's sorrowful song. He rose, naked and dripping water. The house jerked again, harder this time. Something clomped across the roof. He tied on his robe and wiped the shaving cream off the unshaven left half of his face.

When he flung open the door, the house lurched again and knocked him backward. A shelf in the family room crashed. Glass sprinkled across floor. He crab-walked down the hall instead. The Shut-In's room had a window that faced the backyard. He scrabbled backward on aching palms and feet until his shoulders nudged the closed door.

He crawled inside and sniffed. The room stank of musty sweat and candle wax and beneath that the slippery scent of something dead. Enough sunlight seeped through the drawn blinds over the bed to show him an array of coastal maps, sketches, and handwritten poems covering almost every inch of wall space. Red pins marked spots along the ocean's shore on the maps. The sketches showed bizarre creatures emerging from the sea—massive beasts with tentacles and many furrowed eyes and spiky scales and bloated sacs. Some spewed fire. Others wielded long barbed whips. Printouts from chat rooms gave instructions for strange recipes and bizarre rituals.

Wrinkling his nose, he climbed onto the bed to open the window. The mattress groaned. When he pulled up the blinds, his heart twitched.

His brain whirled in his skull.

No land. No houses. No cars. No neighbors.

His home floated freely upon the ocean. In the sky, swirling storm clouds threatened to swallow the low-hanging sun.

Where had the world gone?

He fell sideways, striking something rigid covered by the blanket. It felt like—holy shit—a leg.

His heart hammered even harder, which seemed impossible. His trembling hand pulled back the thick blanket. The stink of death intensified. Keith's face stared upward with dull eyes at the ceiling. He grabbed his friend's shoulder and his exposed innards squished and sloshed below. He fell off the bed and slammed onto the floor.

At the same time, something crashed out in the living room, followed by heavy footsteps. He looked down the hall in time to see an inhuman silhouette come into view. Alien voices exchanged syllables that sounded like drunken whale songs. Head spinning, he scooted backward under the bed.

Footsteps hurried down the hall. Two pairs of alien feet shuffled into view—scaly flippers stuffed into wooden slippers. The contents of a shelf crashed to the ground. More drunken whale song.

Murphy's eyes went wide. He tried to slow his breathing, but his lungs were fiery pistons. He squeezed his hands into fists. The grisly image of Keith's corpse kept flashing behind his eyes.

A cool hand rested on the back of his neck. He almost screamed.

A voice behind him said, "It's okay. They can't hear you. They're practically deaf up here above the sea."

He flinched with each word, expecting the monsters to yank the bed upward and cut him open like a fish. Like Keith. But if the creatures heard the voice, they didn't show it.

"Is that you?" he said, struggling to remember the Shut-In's name.

"What's left of me."

"What happened to Keith? What are those things? What the hell is going on?"

"I offered Keith to Gwanvobitha. It was necessary to complete the Summoning. The Undying Lord has blessed our world with his appearance. Unfortunately, our god has rivals. Ours was not the only Summoning. The battle is done. Now we wait for the gods to rise again, for no god ever truly dies. That which has no birth can have no real death."

While the Shut-In ranted, Murphy turned his head—scalp and jaw wedged between box spring and floor. He almost gasped when he saw his housemate. All color had been drained from his face, which now leered back at him with eyes sunk deep into the skull. When he spoke, teeth fell out of his mouth and sprinkled on the floor.

"What the hell happened to you?"

"I was going to be remade in our Undying Lord's image, but now that image rots. I am a ruin, but you, you will fare well in this new world."

"What did you do to me last night?"

"Fare well."

"What did you do to Keith?"

"Fare well," the Shut-In shouted.

"Shut up," he whispered.

The deranged sub-leaser shoved the bottom of the bed upward so that it slammed back against the floor. His pale lips retracted into a rictus smile. An incisor popped free. Flipper feet clomped across the floor.

"Fare well," his housemate said again.

A slippery tentacle latched onto Murphy's ankle. Terror boiled over in his chest. He tried to kick free but was yanked backward. He was now halfway out from under the bed. At any moment, he expected his exposed legs to be stabbed, pummeled, or crushed. Panic swarmed in his skull. He grabbed the Shut-In's wrist. The bones inside the feverish flesh crackled beneath Murphy's grip.

The Shut-In's smile collapsed into a sneering grin. He giggled or perhaps sobbed, impossible to tell which.

"Fare well."

"Damn you," Murphy said. "Help me."

"I already have."

Murphy squeezed even harder. Another tentacle gripped his other ankle. The creatures tugged. Something jabbed into his ribs, and pain flared inside him. The Shut-In's wrist collapsed, now no bigger than a twig. His grip slid downward past the wrist to the hand, in which fragile bones snapped and popped.

"Fare well."

The creatures yanked again. He lost his grip. They lifted Murphy into the air. He flopped and flailed, now face-to-face with one of the creatures. Its face was a slimy mosaic of ridged shells crammed inside a disco ball-sized glass bowl filled with seawater. Seaweed braids floated along either side of its face. Shells and glistening muscles made up its torso, which sat perched upon what looked like two massive lobster tails. Six chunky arms protruded from its sides, each holding mucky blades forged from long spines and cemented upon a guard made of coral and shell. It stank of fish and sewage.

They hustled him out the front door, where a bizarre sailing vessel was moored. Several masts protruded like spines from its multiple decks, which seemed to be composed of bones and wood and frozen sand. Leathery sails drooped from the masts.

He'd not see the sun again for a terribly long while.

*

In the bowels of the ship, the creatures strapped him to a table and pressed a red-hot branding iron to the shaven right side of his face.

Searing heat burst upon his cheek, echoed by the invisible tattoos simmering on his hands and feet. He bucked and screamed. When the Faithful pulled the iron away, bits of charred flesh clung to it. The scent of burnt skin stabbed his nostrils.

They flipped him onto his belly, forced a slick leathery sack over his head, and bound his hands behind his back. Something wet and slippery slid over his left pinky, and he feared that this was some kind of alien foreplay. They yanked the wetness away, tearing his pinky nail with it and leaving behind only the torn nail bed and searing agony. He screamed into his sack.

A rattling noise that he'd come to recognize as laughter echoed in the darkness.

The slipperiness slid over his left ring finger.

"Please," he said. "Don't."

One by one, they ripped the nails from his fingers and toes. When it was done, tentacles and flippers lifted him into the stuffy air. Wood and metal groaned and clicked all around him. He could feel no breeze and so assumed himself to be in the belly of the horrid ship.

The beasts tossed him into nothingness. His head spun. His belly twirled. He landed sideways on something at once hard and soft. Someone gasped beneath him. He'd landed on a pile of bodies, some alive and others as lifeless as sacks of rice. A guttural groan emitted from the person he'd landed on. He grasped with his bound hands, clutching first soft belly and then softer breast. A woman. She grunted and twisted away.

"I'm sorry," he said.

She responded only with slurred grunts and weeping. Dread sloshed in his veins as he imagined what they'd done to her. Broken her jaw? Cut out her tongue? More groans and sobs peppered the darkness. Fear and nausea tangled in his belly and bubbled up his throat. He dry-heaved into the bag covering his head.

*

The ship sailed on.

Minutes stretched into hours into days, punctuated only by the door creaking open. Sometimes, their captors would stab him in the spine with something sharp and hot. It seemed like torture at first but later he decided it must've been some kind of nutrition. Other times, the monsters dropped fresh captives onto the pile. Some could still speak.

"It started with a shooting at an orphanage in Seattle," an insurance agent from Kansas City said, "and then news broke of several synchronized killings in Japan. Next was Portugal. The reporters called it terrorism at first."

"I was up late playing Mortal Kombat online," said a female substitute teacher from Denver, "when suddenly my opponent vanished mid-match. I got up to get a drink and happened to check the news. Cellphone footage had leaked from a crime scene in Charleston. Gruesome images of bloody pentagrams and other symbols."

A cafeteria worker from Hickam Air Force Base in Honolulu was woken by a call from his boyfriend. "He said the whole base was on alert, that some disturbance had been detected in both the Pacific and Atlantic Oceans. When I lost the call, I turned on the t.v. and saw about all the murders. Then there was footage captured from the Atlantic Ocean. A giant claw rose upward. There were tsunami warnings. And then my apartment was floating in the water. Whatever magic kept it from sinking also kept the water running."

Day after day, the prisoners existed in dank darkness. Hunger gnawed at Murphy's stomach. The prisoners took shifts sleeping on top of one another in the narrow hole. Not all survived the journey. Corpses made decent enough beds if you broke the bones just right.

*

After what must have been weeks, an abrupt shudder wracked the whole vessel. The door above creaked open, and he braced for either another falling prisoner or a shot in the spine. Instead, something slimy and long wrapped around him and hoisted him upward.

"What's happening?" he said. "Please stop."

His fellow prisoners offered similar pleas and questions and prayers. He was carried onward, first through cold draft—fresh air— then into stifling heat.

Slimy hands unbound his hands and spread his arms wide. His muscles screamed. His captors hung him spread-eagled upon a rough wall. At long last, the bag was removed from his head.

His starved eyes nearly gagged on the dim light. He squinted into the face of a monster, except this one wore goggles and not a glass bowl. Black tubes ran from its nostrils to gills at its neck. Shiny scales covered its sunken belly.

He was still wearing what was left of his bathrobe, and they'd strapped him to the inner wall of a circular shaft. The monster in front of him stood on a narrow wooden catwalk that circled the diameter of the shaft. Other catwalks were anchored below and above, and more than a dozen humans—some naked, others clothed—were hung upon the walls at each level. The catwalks were made of salvaged wood and metal, but the shaft's wall felt soft and rough like a cat's tongue.

The monsters anchored other humans to the curved wall on either side of him. Most of the creatures had glass globes on their heads, but some wore goggles and tubes. When they'd bound the final prisoner, the monsters each pulled a thick hose out of the wall and spoke into them, their voices slippery and slurry and amplified in the chamber.

"Welcome to the Pain Engine. You who are not among the Faithful will now suffer for our Lord Glandrictial. You will resurrect that which cannot be killed, that which is ever unborn and thus ultimately eternal."

"Wait," he said. "Please."

The Faithful ignored him. It held the hose in front of him. A sharp barb protruded from its end, like three fishing hooks held together by rust.

"This is your connection to your new God," they said. "Now you will worship at the altar of suffering."

It punched him in the gut and he gasped. The Faithful shoved the tube between his teeth. He tried biting down, but it wiggled down his throat like a thick worm. He choked and convulsed and sputtered as it undulated inside him and twisted into his gut. All around him, his fellow prisoners writhed and whimpered and gagged.

The tube's movements ceased. He hung limp and sweaty on the wall. His neighbors eventually went still, too. The only noise was vague squirming in the dark levels above and below.

"From the watery ashes of your world, your new god will live again and still and always," the Faithful said. "Give yourself wholly to this holy blessing." After a beat, they said, "Amen."

A storm of agony raged instantly inside him, a blender razing his insides and chewing at his secret nooks and crannies. He screamed around the tube. They all did, and the tubes amplified the screams in the shaft so that the noise cut into his brain. Blood dripped from his ears.

*

The agony continued day after day. He could only gauge time by the thickening of his beard, which sprouted slowly only from the unbranded half of his face.

The hateful tube in his gut must've provided some form of nourishment, because he didn't die from dehydration, though hunger constantly lurked beneath the sharper pains stabbing inside him. Usually the Hurt—which is what he came to call the hose—stayed in his gut. Other times, it burrowed into his thighbones or choked his tender lungs or probed inside his groin. It was a like a miner searching constantly for uncharted pockets of suffering.

When the Hurt touched him in a special new way, his spine tensed and he screamed around the tube and his ears throbbed and his bladder drizzled what little it held. The Hurt rarely let him sleep, keeping him on the fringes of lunacy. He had conversations with long-dead pets. He saw rain where there was none—purple fat globs of gleaming liquid.

By the time his half beard tickled his chest, a Faithful yanked the Hurt out of his face. He tried to curse at his tormentors but could only croak a few syllables.

His captors pulled him and the other prisoners off of the wall. The others fell to the catwalk like ragdolls. He somehow had the strength to stand but let himself topple. The Faithful stacked them on a cart and as they were wheeled away, other Faithful hosed down the now bare wall.

They dumped the prisoners inside a deep, gated trench that stank of rot. He crawled over twitching flesh and feeble bones, uselessly cocked elbows and pointless hipbones.

"Finish him," said the female substitute teacher from Denver, her voice now shredded. "Fatality." He saw her break the arm of her dead neighbor—a compound fracture that she used to carve a jagged gash in her own throat.

Later, he used her belly as a pillow and fell into deep sleep until a tentacle raised him out of the trench. The Faithful sorted the prisoners into two piles—living and dead. He was apparently among the living, and tossed onto a cart whose wheels squeaked like mice.

The Faithful lifted him back onto the wall along with his fellow survivors and a new batch of recruits.

"Welcome to the Pain Engine," the Faithful said.

*

Time stretched onward. His beard grew past his pectoral muscles which inexplicably bulged larger. It was as though the Hurt was feeding off of him, but his tattooed palms and feet were somehow siphoning strength from it, as well.

With each new visit to the trenches, he found himself surrounded by scrawny bodies and yet he grew stronger, arms now toned and hard like wet rope. The prisoners with which he'd first arrived had all died.

In the trenches, he first tasted human flesh. It was the first pleasure he'd known since forever, and he swallowed mouthfuls of thigh until his belly ached. Later, he took other pleasures from his fellow prisoners. Some women seemed to enjoy it, though he preferred when they resisted. He clutched them with tingling palms and afterwards wept for his lost humanity.

He feared that the Faithful would realize how long he'd endured and how strong he'd become, but soon realized that he was just cattle to them—another faceless cog in their god-making machine.

When his half beard reached past his pale chiseled abdomen, he conjured a foolish plan. He sought neither meat nor sex in the trenches. No, now he needed guts.

He tore the intestines out of a man with the Ohio state flag tattooed on his forearm. He stretched them on the thick bars covering a drainage hole and left the drawn gut tied in the trench.

Another cycle passed.

He twisted the gut strands together to make six long strings and polished them with a human heart.

Another cycle passed.

He constructed a small instrument using a hipbone and spine. He sorted through the many bones of a woman's hand to find a suitable pick.

The Pain Engine had two doors—one leading to the trenches and one through which new prisoners entered. That door remained open only long enough for the cartload of new cattle to enter—a narrow window of opportunity.

The two doors stood at opposite sides of the shaft. He'd have to fight all the way around, and there were never less than a dozen Faithful on hand.

Hence, the Gore Guitar.

*

The last time the Faithful took him from the trenches, he'd stuffed pieces of tongue into either ear and tucked the guitar inside his tattered robe. They tossed him on the cart. The wheels whined below him as it shuddered down the tunnel. The Pain Engine's door sludged open. The cart passed through. More than a dozen Faithful waited to mount their meat upon the wall.

Time to rock these motherfuckers.

He clutched the Gore Guitar and leapt off the cart. Guards bellowed. He shoved a scrawny prisoner at the nearest Faithful. They fell in a heap. He yanked the Hurt out of the wall and shoved the tube onto the guitar strings.

Bone pick in hand, he struck a series of notes—an amplified screech that made the walls tremble. Even with his makeshift earplugs, the piercing song still jabbed into his brain. The prisoners screamed. The guards wearing fishbowls fell on hands and knees. The ones with goggles clutched their heads.

He kept strumming. His forearms ached. His fingertips burned. Soon blood made the guitar strings slippery.

The guards staggered closer, brows furrowed.

He dropped to one knee and strummed with all his might. Sweat poured off his face. The closest guard unsheathed a spiny sword. It lurched closer, its shadow now sliding over him. Please. Please. His right hand blurred with concentrated motion. His left fingers probed and pressed strings, hoping to find the note that would bring his salvation.

The guard raised the sword. Murphy kept on strumming.

All at once, the globes covering the majority of the guards' heads shattered. Glass and stank water sprayed in all directions, tinkling over his shoulders and stinging the back of his neck. The guard thrust his sword downward, but he lurched sideways and swung the Gore Guitar upward. The evil instrument shattered in a mess of strings. The guard spilled backward off the catwalk but not before Murphy relieved him of his sword.

Most of the guards now lay on the catwalk gulping uselessly at the dry air. Only four with goggles remained upright, and one stood closest to the exit doorway, in which a suffocating guard now lay twitching and gasping.

With a roar, Murphy fought his way toward the exit, stabbing and slashing. He felled the first guard. The fresh prisoners on the cart writhed and wrestled, but they were bound and of little help now. The second guard held up a short spear. Murphy charged, slamming the creature into the wall, stabbing him in the gut and snatching his weapon. He pivoted and threw the spear at the guard in the doorway. It struck him between the shoulder blades. He fell to the ground, bellowing a mournful song.

The fourth guard blew into a small spiral shell, which issued a deep note. Murphy stabbed the guard through the throat, but too late. The warning note already echoed throughout the Pain Engine. More guards would be coming.

He unbound the prisoners on the cart, a motley crew of four men and two women all with dirty hair, squinting eyes, sunburnt flesh, and many scars.

"Grab weapons," he said. "We need to go now."

He led them down the passage, a sword clasped in each pulsating hand. The first wave of guards attacked, and he dived amongst them like a man possessed, which in fact he supposed he was, because his feet and hands throbbed with vengeance seasoned by eons and spread across hundreds of worlds, and he knew himself to be a pawn in an ancient war but even a pawn can be the difference between victory and defeat. He decapitated one of the creatures with a ferocious slice of his blade and—grasping its still-twitching tentacles—used its skull as a mace until it was nothing but pulpy brain and bone fragments.

When the first battle was done, only three of the refugees remained fit enough to stand. One of the women had suffered a slash to the thigh and lay bleeding on the floor. He stabbed her in the eye—her remaining eye going all wide and staring stupidly at the blade—and ordered the others to follow him.

*

The guards seemed ill-equipped for resistance, for at every turn Murphy was greeted with looks of panic and surprise. He stumbled soon upon a kind of processing area where newly-arrived humans were being branded and bagged and bound and relieved of their fingernails. He liberated them and dispatched their tormentors.

"Come on, dammit," he said, hating the grit in his Hurt-ravaged throat.

In the end, he led a band of perhaps twenty refugees through a narrow tube onto the surface of their prison. He expected to inhale fresh air but the outside smelled of rotten fish and sour rain. He expected sunlight and blue skies but instead found a half moon hanging crooked amongst green glowing stars. A strange haze hung in the sky, not eclipsing the stars but tainting them the color of pea soup. Their prison, he discovered, was the floating corpse of whatever god those idiots had chosen to worship. The dead thing sprawled so large that he was unable to see the full scope of it. If he had to guess, he'd imagine it larger than Manhattan.

He'd later learn that this god was one of several to have risen from some otherworldly portal beneath the ocean depths. Their immense bodies had flooded the globe—like a fat man plopped into a bathtub—and their corpses, along with the wreckage of human civilization, had soiled the seamless world-ocean.

The god's flaccid tentacles sprawled outward for miles. Armored platelets the size of skyscrapers sunk into its festering flesh.

An assortment of houses and apartment buildings and even a barn floated inexplicably in the water, all lashed together with thick rope and docked beside the god's corpse. His own home drifted among them. The same alien vessel that had been docked at his house floated on the edge of this strange conglomeration.

Schools of dead fish drifted in the water, eyes shriveled and mouths agape. Flocks of flightless birds floated amongst them, wings spread and torn like flightless angels.

"We're going back for the others," he said.

A thin man with a shaggy beard shook his head. "I won't go back in there."

The others murmured wary agreement. Anger swirled inside Murphy. In truth, he didn't care about the tortured souls inside the Pain Engine, but he needed a larger crew and couldn't gather them alone. So, he did what he did best—he wrote himself a script.

"Humanity may be near extinction," he said. "Our brothers and sisters inside this corpse prison may be all that's left. If we turn our backs on them, we may be turning traitor upon all humanity. This may be our only chance to save them from a life of suffering to feed the god whose Faithful have already taken so much from us. I, for one, cannot live with this weight pressed upon my soul."

He almost laughed at these last words, for he knew that soul had long ago been crushed into a flimsy remnant.

"You can grab an oar and paddle for your freedom or you can take a sword and fight for humanity's salvation." He held up his bloody swords. The crowd fidgeted. He needed to close strong. He placed a hand over his chest. "Hold that choice in your heart. Let the answer echo in your veins."

The bloodied and bleak crowd stared back at him, swaying upon the gigantic corpse. Diseased waves clapped upon the sagging god flesh. A seagull flew toward them from the endless ocean and crashed upon the decaying shore. It flopped and flailed before finding peace.

*

On the New Theatre's well-lit stage, a dove—not a ragged seagull—flies over the assembled actors. It does not collapse but instead soars over the delighted crowd. The actor portraying

Halfbeard places a hand—Pledge of Allegiance style—over his bulging chest and says, "Hold that choice in your heart, brothers and sisters, and let the answer echo in your veins."

The words boom amongst the makeshift bleachers forged from iron and driftwood—now perches for a motley assortment of god miners, children, fishermen, city divers, and deity farmers.

Halfbeard himself sits deep in the audience. His tattered cloak hangs heavy with saltwater and more than a little blood. The wounds in his chest throb angrily. His damned hands and feet chew upon the pain, feeding it back to him.

He chuckles at the play and munches on a sliver of god jerky. The actor portraying him does a decent enough job and his bathrobe costume is shockingly similar to the real article. During one fight scene, his half-beard hangs loose from his face, but the audience appears too engrossed in the legend to care.

The writers of this farce have given him a love interest—a fierce dark-haired woman who serves as first mate in his many celebrated pirate adventures. Together, they and his loyal crew go on to kill many Faithful and save countless human lives. His bride is slain at the end of the first act by his nemesis, a Faithful General who nearly kills Halfbeard with a sinister trap involving submarines and dolphins.

In real life, he never had a bride. He took many lovers over the course of his travels—some willing and others not—but none lasted long. He never had a first mate, and his allegedly loyal crew consisted of mercenaries and criminals and slaves.

Nor did he have a nemesis.

He did survive countless assassination attempts, including tonight's attack. And he still harbors a deep mistrust of dolphins. He did kill hundreds of Faithful, but also murdered countless humans and left only their corpses to tell the tale to nibbling fishes.

Halfway through the second act, his mood darkens. The actor on stage seems to mock his horrid existence. The cheers of the assembled audience only serve to anger him and exacerbate his self-loathing. No longer having an appetite, he hands the last of his god jerky to the child sitting next to him, pats the girl's head, and strides out toward Lunar Acres' cramped alleys.

"You're leaving?" says the theatre worker manning the rear exit, a scruffy young man with neck tattoos and a hooked nose. "But the end has yet to come."

Halfbeard shakes his hooded head. "I fear the end will never come."

"It's an inspiring tale, isn't it?" the worker says. "I know it's impossible, but I like to think Halfbeard is still out there—still sailing the seas and plaguing the Faithful and watching over all of us."

"Why's it impossible?"

"He'd be a hundred years old by now, hardly in any condition to hurt anyone."

"You'd think so, wouldn't you?" Halfbeard says. "What about the incident earlier tonight? I heard the Faithful attacked a man that looked like Halfbeard."

He shrugs. "Hard to say. Could have been street actors. Could have been one of the Halfbeard impostors. I've seen whole gangs of them, dumb kids with faces covered in tattoos and lame braided half-beards. No, he's dead. He lives only in our hearts."

"Tell me, son, what would you say to Halfbeard if you met him in these very streets on this very night?"

"Oh, I'd pat his back and thank him dearly for his many sacrifices."

"And what would you offer him?"

The worker purses his chapped lips. "Whatever he wanted, I reckon."

"Indeed."

Halfbeard punches the man in the throat, crushing the tender bits that would vocalize a cry for help. He drags his victim flailing into a dark alley. The shadows stink of piss and rot. He wraps his throbbing hands over the worker's neck and squeezes. The fool's sunburnt face darkens. His eyes bulge.

All the while, the flesh of Halfbeard's palms and feet tingle deliciously. He's learned over the years not to gulp such meals like a hungry wolf, rather to sip the pain and fear. In doing so, he turns this man's life from a meal into a banquet. Like a civilized man, he even uses a knife and fork.

As Halfbeard probes intestines with rusty tines, the victim twitches and convulses. In the distance, the audience cheers and claps and stamps their feet. His head goes all dizzy. The applause intensifies. He imagines the actors must be taking their bows. Perhaps the lead kisses his slain bride or feigns one final jab at his nemesis.

"Such things as heroes and villains are myths," Halfbeard says to the bloody mess below him. "The real evil lurks inside us. It whispers under our beds and itches in our palms and dances beneath our feet."

The mess squirms in response.

"Don't worry. We're almost done."

Soon the crowd flows past. Boys and girls stab at each other with poorly made toy swords sold by the theatre. Men and women walk hand-in-hand, talking through wide smiles. When the last of them passes by and the lights of the New Theatre blink out, he clutches the man's heart, embracing the final jerky beats.

"Is this where I live?" he says. "Here in your heart?"

The man shudders one last time. He tosses what's left of him into the ocean's greedy froth, pocketing his victim's measly five scales.

He walks through dark streets to his old house, docked at the edge of Lunar Acres. His boots clomp over the roof, down the ladder, and onto the porch. From there, the ocean stretches endlessly in search of the sky. The two only ever meet in dreams.

The house stinks of death, no matter how much he cleans. It's as though the space is haunted by the stench of his deeds. He could've moved a long time ago. Lord knows he can afford it, but it seems appropriate to stay here. Sometimes while napping on the couch, he can recall the man he once was before the world succumbed to the wrestling of alien gods. He undresses and takes the pilfered scales to Keith's old room. He places them in a bulging fabric bag and updates his ledger. His fortune is obscene, filling the rooms formerly occupied by both Keith and the Shut-In.

At last, he settles into his bed. His old bathrobe—long ago converted into a pirate sash and covered with sloppy stitches and random patches—hangs on the wall.

Sleep claims him quickly.

He wakes up only once in the night hearing a kind of squishy shuffling in the darkness. His tired eyes probe the shadows. Across the hall, a pale puddle of flesh glistens in the greenish moonlight. It slides closer. Dread grips his spine.

The thing grins and whispers, "Go back to sleep. Forget."

He means to grab his sword, but his palms and feet go numb,

betraying him and anchoring him to the bed. His vision darkens. He hears the beast slide closer, now murmuring gibberish chants. Its flesh slides over him, cold and oily. He cannot scream. It whispers to him all night as it does its horrid work.

An eternity later, dawn drags itself out of the drowned world's soggy edges. Halfbeard sits up and gasps. He staggers into the living room and opens the door. The world ocean licks at his porch. As always, the memory of last night's visitation fades out. The low hanging sun crawls across his face, where a solitary tear withers and dries on his cheek. It leaves behind a salty trail.

The Cat and the Goldfish

The raindrops hammer the ground, but not loud enough to drown out my brother Theo's solemn voice. "... He was more than a friend. He was more than his size. He watched as I grew up under his eyes. His words were a blessing, his advice solid built. His memory a flower never to wilt..."

We're standing in the backyard of our childhood home, where Theo, though older than me, still lives. Theo wrote the eulogy on an extra-long yellow legal pad. He's now on the fifth page. I roll my eyes.

"For fuck's sake, Theo. He was a goldfish. I loved him, too, but can we just get on with this?" It's not that I wasn't fond of the Goldfish. Despite his constant fretting and general high-strung nature, the little-finned runt was a great friend. It's just that Theo has a way of making any situation...difficult.

Theo uses a little green fish net to scoop the lifeless fish out of its bowl. Even dead, the Goldfish's scales are beautiful, the sort of orange that would usher the evening's sun into the horizon. Bowing his head, Theo drops the fish into an open cigar box—it lands with a wet flop—and places the box into the shoebox-sized hole. So meticulous, my brother. Always so meticulous.

I smell something reminiscent of cinnamon coming from Mom's herb garden. The pentagon-shaped patch of earth is overgrown with waist-high, thorny weeds. Theo was never much of a gardener.

He stares at me with his faded, dull eyes, even as he continues the eulogy. "Swimming his laps in his clear glass bowl, he was a goldfish with soul. I'll miss his wide eyes and smile, his willingness to swim that extra mile."

Son of a bitch. The legal pad's just a prop. He's making it up as he goes. I sigh and begin tossing dirt into the hole.

"Sally, that's just rude. I never thought you to be so crude."

"No, *rude* is using a goldfish's death to get a captive audience for your half-assed poetry jam."

"If I wanted a captive to stay here," says Theo between gritted teeth, "I could have one right away, my dear."

It's an odd thing to say, but that's always been Theo's way. Dammit. Now he has me doing it.

I pull my hair out of my eyes. "So, have you seen *him* lately? Since Mom died?"

Theo doesn't look at me. Instead he shovels scoops of dirt into the grave with a plastic red shovel. The rain intensifies, spraying droplets of mud on our jeans.

"No," he says. "I haven't seen *him* in months, maybe years. And believe me, over it I'm not shedding tears."

The *him* in question is a five-foot talking cat that used to harass the two of us when Mom was away, barging in on our lives and causing no small manner of mischief.

Mom was an odd one. She wore lots of red and black, and had more boyfriends than I can count on fingers and toes. As a result, we grew up with many "dads." Mom was what most would call, I suppose, a witch. That's how it is that we grew up with a talking goldfish. That's how it is, I imagine, that we had random encounters with a talking cat. And that's how it is that I've come home from college to attend the Goldfish's funeral.

*

That evening, Theo and I sit in the living room. The room hasn't changed much in the past two decades. The carpet is still blue, though ragged and stained. The mirror that once hung over the fireplace is missing, leaving behind only a slightly askew rectangle of less-faded paint. I wonder if Theo broke the mirror during one of his tantrums.

I'm trying to read my Western Civ homework, but Theo keeps talking at me. "So, how is it?" he asks. "College, I mean. Do you fancy your classes? Are your teachers keen?"

"If you'll stop rhyming, Theo, I'll answer you. But I'm not going to sit here and have a conversation like this."

"It gets lonely here without Mom around," he says. He's wearing just a shirt and pants now, and I can see that he's lost weight. The skin around his eyes is grey, like the burnt, cloudy color of an old glass candleholder.

"There," I say, "now that's what I'm talking about. Let's have a real talk like real people."

"I can hear her breath behind every sound," he finishes. "Her shadow, it seems, is ever near. I see her crying in the mirror."

I want to tell him to shut the fuck up, but I know exactly what he's saying. In fact, I thought that very same thing when I stared into the bathroom mirror earlier today. My eyes were red and puffy, but they still looked like Mom's. Theo and I both have her eyes.

"You miss her a lot, huh?" I ask.

"It's a lot harder being the one who remains. I'm covered in memories like blood-splattered stains."

I roll my eyes. So, this is what it's all been building toward. He's laying the guilt on me for leaving town. And he gets to be the brave martyr who stayed behind to handle the family affairs.

"So, fucking leave, Theo. Get the hell out of this little town."

"But it's so pretty. And I hate the city."

"So find *another* little town. They're all over the place, you know."

He shrugs.

"There's nothing left to stay here for. You need to find your own path, Theo." He says nothing. I sigh and stand. "I've got to crash. I have a long drive tomorrow."

"You're so far away," he says, "the better part of a day."

I stomp down the hall, shaking my head and clenching my fists. I could really use a beer. Naturally, Theo only has wine.

On the way to my room, I stop and stare at one of the many framed pictures in the hallway, one of Mom and a short, wide-eyed man. She's much younger, just about my age now. The picture must have been taken before I was born. Even before Theo was born. She's wearing a black halter top with red lace trim. Her smile looks hungry. The man she's with looks excited and uneasy, like he's just tasted the best pastry in the world, and he knows it's about to devour him in return.

I glance into Theo's room as I pass. As it's always been, the room is immaculately tidy. The spines of every book are lined up flush with each other. The bed is neatly pressed. His drawings and writings are neatly stacked on the desk, probably organized by subject matter. My eyes tear up to see that he's put the fish bowl, still filled with water, back on his nightstand.

When I get to my room, it's exactly as I'd left it. The same thorny flowers painted on the mirror. The same black satin comforter on the bed.

As I fall asleep, the picture of my mom floats in my memory. She looked so different then. So carefree and, well, naughty. A far cry from the woman who raised me, so intimidating in her scarlet red overcoat and black high heels. I remember the noise those heels made as she walked across the driveway. *Clack. Clack. Clack.*

Gradually, my thoughts flicker into dreams.

*

Tap. Tap. Tap. Well into the night, the noise wakes me. It sounds like rain dripping from a leaky rain gutter, but it's coming from inside the house. I listen with my eyes in the dark, searching the shadows for movement.

Tap. Tap. Tap. The sound is coming from under the bed, I soon realize. My heart flutters. Swallowing hard, I slowly lean over the bed and look underneath. But it's empty, except for my old combat boots. The sound must be coming from the basement.

Tap. Tap. Tap. I get out of bed and slide my feet into the boots. They always made me feel stronger. I pull the laces tight and walk out of the room. Theo's bedroom door is closed. I'm still pissed enough that I don't even consider knocking on it.

Tap. Tap. Tap. The basement door protests even as it opens. I tip-toe down the wooden, splintered steps. At the bottom of the stairs is a shelf filled with glass mason jars, each labeled in mom's flowing handwriting. The rest of the basement is piled high with dusty memories of our youth: our tennis racquets, Theo's bike, a crooked rake, the toy boat that never floated, and the rubber ball with the white star. Leaning shelves hold rows of the thick, leather-bound books my mother collected, the brittle pages handwritten in dead languages. I see fresh fingerprints in the dust on the jackets. Past the shelves are the tool bench and pegboard, where I'm disturbed to see the outlines of several missing implements: a saw, pliers, and a hammer.

Tap. Tap. Tap. At the end of the basement is the bomb shelter, and that's where I see the Cat. Somehow, I manage not to scream.

Tap. Tap. Tap. Each of the Cat's wrists is bound by a rusty, thick chain anchored to the bomb shelter's sidewalls. The chains are the only thing keeping the Cat from falling. His fur is matted with blood. Patches of hair are missing, revealing purple and smoke-colored bruises. He's still wearing the same red and white striped hat, though it's stained and crumpled. The Cat is smaller than I'd remembered. Of course, I was much younger then.

Tap. Tap. Tap. Scattered on the floor are several sticky, dark tools: a saw, pliers, and a hammer. Behind the Cat, propped against the wall, is the mirror missing from upstairs. It reflects his back, a crisscrossing of lacerations over bruised flesh. Poking out of the fingertip of one blood-soaked glove is a sharp claw. The claw taps against the chain.

Tap. Tap. Tap.

I clear my throat.

Tap. Tap.

The Cat looks up slowly, like a night orchid opening itself for the moon's shine. Finally, he says, "It's been a while. A long while."

"I went away to school. Did . . . Did my brother do this to you?"

"Yes," he hisses, because it would be too painful to nod.

"Why? God in heaven and hell, why?"

"I don't know," he says, because it would be too agonizing to shrug. "Please. Please let me go."

I step closer. "I want to. But how do I know Theo doesn't have good reason to lock you up?"

"And torture me? Tell me, Sally. Tell me a good reason to torture a person."

"You're not a person," I say.

"I was once."

I stare into the Cat's eyes. Gone are the things I remember most: mischief and humor. All that remains is honesty.

The hammer is heavy in my hands. I use the sharp end to pry the chain out of the concrete wall. It comes free with a satisfying pop of dust and crumbs, and the Cat tumbles to the floor.

"I . . ." he says. "That is, we, we can take it from here."

With the rusty chain still dangling from his wrist, the Cat pulls his hat off his head. I know who he's looking for: the twenty-six cats that live under his hat, each smaller than the last, each hiding in the hat of the preceding cat.

I scream when the Cat lifts his hat. Underneath sits a bruised and lifeless miniature cat—what's left of A. Like the original Cat, A wears a red and white-striped hat, only his tiny hat has a bold letter "A" across the front. But A isn't breathing. For a moment, everything is still and silent. Then A slumps over on the Cat's head.

From underneath A's hat, a smaller cat corpse, its hat labeled "B," spills downward. B flops on the Cat's shoulder—its neck at a twisted angle. Then yet another, even smaller, cat C spills out—this one missing its legs.

And so it goes. One after another, the Cat picks up each lifeless body, tips its hat off, and discovers yet another body. By the time he gets to "W," the corpses are too small to see and the floor is covered in blood.

"Wh-why would Theo do this?" I ask.

Tears spill out of the Cat's eyes. "He kept asking me . . ." His words trail off into a wet cough. "Over and over, day after day, he asked me the same question: 'Tell me the secret you've told no other. Give me the magic of my mother.'"

"The what?" I ask.

"And when I told him that there was no secret, that I didn't know what he was talking about, he'd hurt me again. And again. And again. He even tried to use the mirror on me."

"What do you mean?" I ask, looking at the mirror and seeing my mother's eyes.

"The mirror is magic, though it doesn't work on animals. It reflects the secret thoughts that you don't want to reveal. Your mom probably used it on you kids when she thought you were lying."

He's right. Whenever Mom questioned us, she'd sit us in the chair by the fireplace—right under the mirror.

I step away from the mirror, catching a glimpse of myself naked, tangled under the sheets with two giggling college friends. "This doesn't make sense," I say. "Why would he do this?"

"Because," says the Cat, "because he found out my secret."

I cross my arms and tap my foot. The Cat continues.

"I was once a man. Your mother and I were . . . involved. This was before you were born. As I'm sure you know, your mother was not the sort to keep men around for very long. This simply was not in her nature. I used to hate her for it, for what she had done to me . . ." He gestured at his furry body.

"You can't be serious," I say. "Mom turned you into a cat?"

The Cat nods. "She was no longer interested in the . . .

romantic aspect of our relationship, but she still wanted to keep me available. For companionship. Of course, rather than a lap cat, she got a five-foot, talking cat. Such is the nature of magic."

"I can't believe . . ." I say.

"I'm not her only former lover to join the animal kingdom."

I lick my lips. "You mean, the Goldfish?"

"Yes," says the Cat. "You're mother was an exceptionally powerful witch. She was—It was difficult for her to have access to so much power at such a young age. As time went on, she grew even more powerful, and fortunately, more responsible."

"What does any of this have to do with Theo?"

"He's somehow under the impression that I can help him to cast spells, gain riches, cheat death. He thinks that I'm keeping him from accessing the magics that are his to claim."

"Are you?"

The Cat shook his head. "I am a creature of magic," he says. "Though it passes through me, I can't control it. I can't use it. And sadly . . ." The Cat coughs blood into his glove. "Sadly, the magic can't help me now."

I can barely look at him. "We have to get you to a hospital."

"Yes, we almost certainly should," says a voice from behind me. "But as ideas go, that isn't so good." Theo.

Gasping, I turn to see Theo standing in the entrance to the bomb shelter. He's holding a rusted knife matted with blood and hair. The Cat hisses—a thick, knotted sound sprayed with blood.

"Of course, medical science won't know what to do," says Theo, "with a magical cat that's black, red, and blue."

"Theo, what's wrong with you?" I ask, surprised to find myself standing defensively between Theo and the Cat. I never even liked the Cat.

"Sally," he says, "there are things at work here, things that are quite beyond your means and ends. Go back to your school, dear, to your mass-produced books, and mass-produced friends."

"You're insane," I say.

Theo steps closer. "This . . . Cat is not worthy of your pity. But if you must feel this way, feel it back in the city."

"Knock it off, Theo. Can't you see that the Cat doesn't know anything? He's not hiding anything from you."

"Oh, I think he's hiding something deep inside. It's time he be inspected, poked, and pried." Theo grins and holds up the knife.

He lunges at me, grabbing me by the hair. Before I know it, he's spun me around and has his forearm under my chin. He's stronger than he looks.

"Theo, please–" I say, but the last word is choked off. The flat edge of his blade is pressed against my temple. Smells like rust and burnt hair.

"Now listen, you Cat," he says, "or there's going to be pain. Tell me how to get magic, or you'll see Sally stain."

I drive my heel down into Theo's foot. He's only wearing slippers, so I'm pretty sure I break a bone or two. His grip loosens as he screams. I turn, elbowing him in the jaw. He pushes me away, takes a few steps back, and picks the hammer up off the ground.

"You meddling little bitch," he says. "Mom was . . .."

But his rhyme is thankfully cut short by the Cat, who lunges at Theo from behind. Though one of the chains still binds him to the wall, the Cat has enough slack to reach Theo. The Cat hisses and digs his claws into Theo's neck. Wincing, Theo screams and swings his hammer backward against the Cat's head.

With Theo distracted, I step forward and kick my combat boot straight into his groin. He falls forward and I kick him again in the side of the head. I take a deep breath, hoping it'll help me stop shaking.

It doesn't.

*

Two pairs of padded handcuffs are still hidden in the back of my closet, right where I'd left them. Enough said.

Theo and the Cat are both unconscious for a long while, long enough for me to fasten the cuffs on Theo's ankles and wrists. I take off the padding first, and then fasten them nice and tight. The veins in Theo's hands begin to bulge almost instantly.

After Theo is bound, I use the hacksaw to take the chains off the Cat's wrists. Aside from an occasional shallow breath, the Cat remains still. I want to call the hospital for the Cat, or the police for Theo, but either option presents the same problem: what will the authorities do with the Cat?

The shadows on the floor, cast through the security glass windows, grow longer as I ponder what to do. Finally, the Cat stirs.

I fight the urge to scratch him behind the ear. "It's me. Sally.

Can you hear me?"

He licks his upper lip. I take that as a yes.

"Look," I say. "I want to help you, but I don't—I'm worried if I take you to the hospital, that—I don't know what they'd do to someone like you. Do you want me to take that risk?"

He whispers something. I lean in closer.

"What?"

"Magic," he says. "Spell. Magic."

"Um . . . M. A. G. I.—"

"You imbecile," says Theo from behind. "He doesn't want another letter. He needs a spell to make him better."

I turn and face Theo. He's struggling with his cuffs, wincing as they dig into his wrists.

"Nobody asked you," I say. "Don't make me get the ball gag." Theo sneers.

"He's right," says the Cat. "The magic is within you, Sally. It is passed from woman to woman, through the generations. It is your birthright. Your gift and your curse."

So. I'm a witch, too. Yee-fucking-haw.

The Cat explains to me that there's a counter-spell that can undo my mom's spell—to make him human again. He says that old magic is a lot like caulk; it gets older and harder with age. So the spell will be brittle and easy to break, but it'll also take a lot of effort to completely scrape away.

I find the spell book on one of the shelves as directed. It's bound with what looks like eel-skin. The pages are made of a yellowish fiber that I don't recognize.

First I gather the ingredients. Most of the herbs are still growing in between the weeds in Mom's garden. I find the other odds and ends—bat wing, dried elk blood, crushed wolf teeth, bear claw shavings, and so on—in the mason jars at the bottom of the steps.

"It's not so much that you have to pronounce the words correctly," says the Cat, "or that you even have to know what they mean. Think of the words as a garden trellis. They are merely the gateway that lets you into the garden. The real work is the planting of the flowers. Or in this case, the pulling of the weeds."

"So, that's what the magic does? It pulls the weeds?"

"No," says the Cat. "*You* pull the weeds. Your will."

"I don't understand."

"Okay, how about this. Think of the words as the sail that you raise to begin a journey."

I stare down at the foreign words on the page. Then I look back up at the cat. "So, what's the wind, then?" I ask. "The magic?" "No, my dear," he says. "*You*. You are the wind. And if you're to unravel this spell completely, you will have to be a raging, mighty gust."

I nod. The spell is before me. The appropriate ingredients are in their proper locations, arranged in a crescent shape arcing around me and the Cat. I clear my throat.

That's when Theo speaks up, "Pardon my intrusion but it seems safe to say that since you're a rookie about to play, perhaps you should practice a little bit first, just in case what's worse becomes worst."

"What's he talking about?" I ask the Cat.

"Magic can be unpredictable at best, Sally," says the Cat. He waves a hand in front of himself, to prove his point. "And in the hands of a novice . . . Well, there's always the chance that the spell could have unintended consequences."

"Well, how am I supposed to practice?" I ask the Cat.

"You can't," he says, "unless you have another victim of the same spell."

The Cat's words pass through my ears. I stare Theo in the eyes, and we have the same thought at the same time. I climb to my feet and walk toward the stairs.

"Sally, the Goldfish is resting in the ground," protests Theo, "where he cannot hear a sound. He's left this painful world behind . . ."

"He's dead," I finish. "He won't mind."

*

A short walk to the backyard and two shovelfuls of mud later, I'm holding a water-logged cigar box in my hand. I take the box into the basement, toss the Goldfish on the floor, and sit.

I chant the words over and over: "Carnitotale. Mirrazorba. Gluni-porous." Gradually, the basement melts away in my vision, becoming a vast ocean. The Goldfish floats on the green water. The waves are tipped with thorns, and they smash into me like a hurricane, leaving gashes on my mind. This is not what I expected.

The Cat's voice echoes in the starless sky, but I can't make out his words. I try to focus on the waves, pushing them away. Gradually, my will becomes a wind, parting the ocean. The Goldfish's corpse falls into the gulf, tumbling to the ocean's floor. Thorny seaweed crawls over the fish. Taking a deep breath, I push harder. The wind strengthens to a full gale, stripping the seaweed away. It grows back as fast as I can remove it.

This goes on for quite awhile.

I push and push until there is no more ocean, no more weeds. Only the basement, the Cat, the Goldfish, and my brother. I realize I'm still chanting. "Carnitotale. Mirrazorba. Gluniporous."

The fish lies there, same as before. My brother laughs. I lower my head.

Then Theo's laughter stops cold. Looking up, I see the Goldfish begin to twitch and bubble, like his scales are boiling. The spell is working.

At first, he begins to swell, like a sponge that's been dipped in water for the first time. Except he grows remarkably bigger. First the size of a cat. Then a dog. Then a small child. All the while, fins melt into hands. A tail splits into feet, then legs. The dead fish is becoming a dead man.

I'm filled with pride until I see the fish-man's reflection in the mirror. My jaw goes limp.

I see a nervous, wide-eyed man in the mirror, the man from the picture in the hall, staring down lovingly at his infant son, Theo.

I see that man years later, now the Goldfish, circling his bowl on my brother's nightstand, whispering little rhymes into Theo's sleeping ears. Planting the seeds of conspiracy, fear, and anger.

I see the Goldfish faking his own death, gills aching inside the cigar box. Waiting with wretched patience for the rain to leak inside.

"You son of a bitch," I say to the fish-man before me. "You manipulated Theo. Your son. You made him think the Cat was his enemy because the Cat stole Mom away from you. You orchestrated all of this, used both of us, to get your revenge and trick me into reversing the spell."

The fish-man giggles, then struggles to stand on his scaly feet. "The hardest part," he gurgles, "wasn't pretending to be dead, but keeping a straight face."

The spell is almost complete. His scales are swollen and

stretched, and they begin popping off to reveal . . . a very old man. His skin is wrinkled and sagging, pocked with sour spots.

"Something's wrong," he says. "I should be in my forties . . . not like this."

"You lived the life of a goldfish," hisses the Cat. "And you aged accordingly in fish years, not people years. Fish only have life expectancies of five or ten years. You were a very old fish. The spell could have been tweaked to account for the difference with some extra dove's tail . . ." For the first time tonight, the Cat has that twinkle in his eye. "I guess I should have mentioned that to Sally."

"Goddamn you," says the fish-man. He tries to kick at the Cat, but something snaps in his hip, sending him sprawling forward through the mirror.

The magical mirror ruptures with a flash of sharp light, and its fragments ripple and tinkle across the floor. A good many of the mirror's shards find their way into the fish-man's neck and chest. He lies on the floor, covered in blood, twitching and gurgling. At the last, only his mouth moves, opening and closing for what seems an eternity.

I can't help but think it appropriate that he dies drowning in his own blood.

*

Theo sobs while I repeat the spell, this time using extra dove's tail, per the Cat's instructions. When the spell is complete, the Cat sheds his hair, loses his tail, and eventually becomes a middle-aged, badly beaten, bloody man. He is quite tall, but is built on a lean frame. I am relieved to see that the twenty-six dead, miniature cats simply disappear. When the transformation is complete, the man smiles weakly at me and nods. I begin to drag him out of the room.

"Sally," says Theo. "You're not just going to leave me here stuck? I didn't mean—I mean, I didn't know–"

"Fuck!" I yell.

Theo jumps. I toss the key to the cuffs just out of his reach. He'll be able to get to it, after a very painful bit of stretching and wiggling.

"But what," says Theo, "what do I do now?"

"Think about what you've done, Theo. Draw it. Write it. Find something redeemable in our story, some way to atone. And make the world better."

These are the last words I say to my brother.

It takes a while to get the battered man to the car. After I ease him into the passenger seat and toss an armful of Mom's books into the trunk, I get inside. "So, what should I call you?" I ask, backing out of the driveway.

"It's too soon for that," he whispers. "I haven't worn my old name in so long, I'm not sure if it'll still fit."

"Theo and the fish were a lot alike, both high strung. Both of them always trying to control everything around them . . ."

"You're not like that at all, are you?" he asks, with a sly grin. "You have a rebellious, mischievous streak in you. A delicious restlessness."

"Yeah," I say. "I can't imagine where I get that from."

"I really couldn't say."

*

That first night in the hospital, I sit by his bed, watching his stomach rise and fall with each breath. I hold his hand, and I swear at least a few times he purrs.

Over the next two weeks, I visit him every day. As he regains his strength, the hospital staff grows increasingly tense. The antics of the patient known only as John Doe soon become the stuff of hospital legend.

Like the time he fills the therapy tubs with Jell-O.

Or the time he cut the rears out of all the surgeon's scrubs. "See how they like waltzing about with their bums hanging out," he says.

Or the time he rides the dinner cart through the pediatric unit.

Of course, whatever the prank, he always sees to it that the resulting mess is cleaned up with surprising ease. Such is his nature.

On the day of his discharge, the staff is both relieved and sad to see him go. I wait by my car as half a dozen nurses wheel him out, laughing and joking all the while. He looks a world of better. He's put on a bit of weight, and his rounded cheeks are a sunset pink.

As we drive away, I clear my throat. "So, have you decided yet? What I should call you, I mean?"

"How about 'Dad'?" he says, as he fiddles with the radio.

"I think I'd like that."

He settles on a rock station, mouthing along with Grace Slick's haunting voice. He begins to pull at his hospital bracelet, which simply reads, "Doe, J."

"I hate these damn things," he hisses. Yes, he hisses.

I wave a hand over his wrist and whisper. The bracelet falls off his wrist, landing on the seat unbroken.

"You've been practicing," he says.

"I still have a long way to go," I say.

"You have no idea, my dear," he says, patting my knee and staring ahead at a road that seems to extend further than the horizon. "Oh, the places you'll go."

The Burning Cycle

The day the world stops going 'round, Rudy's mowing the backyard.

A wide-brimmed hat shades his grey beard. The mower's engine burps along, spraying finely cut grass in his wake. He waves to his neighbor, that asshole Kerry Lipp who pretends not to notice and so he offers a different gesture instead. The Synthe-Bees buzz frantically around the yard, anxious to sip a final drink from the dandelions before the mower lops off their dandy heads. He looks down at the artificial bees and the flowers and envies their quick little lives.

His eyes probe the grass for tendrils of smoke. He shakes his head and takes a drink of his beer. It's been decades and yet he can't stop looking.

Back in the early years of the 21st century, Rudy was biking down a secluded trail when he noticed the ground was burning. Ahead on the left, thick curtains of black smoke wafted out of the strip of grass that ran parallel to the asphalt trail. He'd forgotten his helmet at work and was trying to bike home before dark—balancing the need to go slow because he had no head protection with the urge to go fast to race the setting sun.

When he saw the smoke, he stopped pedaling and let the bike coast while he fumbled for his smartphone. As he closed in on the smoldering earth, he took several pictures.

A lot happened at once. He tried shoving his phone back into his pocket. The smoke raked at his eyes and tickled his nose. The setting sun peeked between some trees and blinded him. He sneezed and coughed. The bike pitched sideways. He lost his balance and tumbled into the grass on the non-smoking side of the blacktop.

His phone clattered upon the trail. Dead leaves scurried past.

The fall clobbered Rudy's knee and scraped the hell out of his elbow.

"Goddammitall," he said, stringing the words together the way his dad used to do whenever he used any kind of tool. "Stupid phone."

He kicked out from under his bike and rubbed his knee. Fortunately, his work pants were in the backpack strapped to the bike. Unfortunately, he'd opted to wear shorts. The fall had scraped a softball-sized patch of skin from his knee. Blood and grit now coated the wound.

Typical. He was just trying to commute to and from work—maybe save the Earth some emissions and get a little exercise—and now he'd screwed up his leg.

It'd been that kind of day. The commute this morning had taken twice as long as he'd anticipated. His boss had glared at him when he walked into the office almost an hour late still wearing his helmet. So, he had to stay an extra hour in the office to make up the time. Now the sun was setting fast, and he knew it'd be dark before he got home. Worse, he'd been in a hurry to leave work—hence, the forgotten helmet—and hadn't yet bothered to phone Heather to tell her he'd be late. He'd planned to stop and call at the next trail intersection.

The smoke drifted past him stinking of burning leaves but darker somehow. Richer. Almost like pipe tobacco. He kicked out from under his bike and retrieved his phone. A spiderweb crack covered the screen, making the screensaver of him and Heather all but unrecognizable. He tried entering his password, but his fingertip slid uselessly over the damaged screen.

Shaking his head, he crossed the trail to examine the fire.

Except he saw no flames—only smoke.

The black stuff rose out of a blackened patch of grass maybe the size of a twin bed. He knelt and ran his hand through the smoke. It was warm but not hot. He brushed his fingers through the charred grass—still not hot enough to burn.

He limped back to his fallen bike—dragging a long shadow behind him—and took the water bottle from its mount. Unscrewing the lid, he poured a bit over the edge of the smoking grass. The ground hissed. The smoke emanating from that spot turned an ashen white for a few moments, then changed back to stormy black.

Up close, it smelled of incense and campfire and cigars and gasoline and cedar chips and barbeque. Of summer nights and road trips, of solitude and languid afternoons. He chugged three swallows of water before screwing the cap back on.

The trail cut between a patch of woods. Through the mostly leafless trees, he could maybe see a few houses, possibly a barn. No other riders appeared to be coming or going along the path. He was alone. No point now trying to race the setting sun. He'd be riding home in the dark for sure. Heather would be pissed, but she wouldn't show it. She'd force a smile. All of her movements would be stiff as if she were being operated by remote control. By bedtime, she'd be over it, though, and they'd likely screw once or twice. She'd gasp his name or God's, and he'd imagine she was someone else.

"I suck," he said to no one at all.

Maybe it was his imagination, but the smoke seemed to twitch in response.

He fished his pack of cigarettes out of his shorts pockets. The pack was heavily dented, and a few of the cancer sticks were broken. He lit the best of the bunch with a disposable lighter and exhaled a stream of white smoke that intertwined with the black smoke.

The dark and light tendrils danced in mid-air like flirty angels—twirling around and around each other.

"Wow," he said. "That's beautiful."

The wind shifted. The black smoke drifted over him like a thick snug blanket on a cold night. The black stuff spoke to him then, not into his ears but somehow it whispered over his skin. Its voice was raspy and throaty. It talked not with words but with undulations. He could smell and taste its ashy vocalizations. It vibrated through him. He could see its voice the way he could sometimes feel music thumping out of a noisy club. It conversed via all of his senses at once, and yet somehow beyond the limits of five senses as if the smoke had wiggled into the synapses of his brain.

It said, "Can I bum one of those?"

As quickly as it came, the voice faded. The smoke shifted upward. He watched it wiggle upward, and took another hit from his cigarette.

Bum one? Had he heard that—felt that—right?

Did the burning grass just ask him for a cigarette? He took one of the broken smokes from the crumpled pack. After removing the filter, he tossed the tobacco and torn paper onto the smoldering ground.

For a moment, the cigarette rested on the blackened grass. Bit by bit, the paper and flecks of tobacco transformed to white ash. He smoked as he watched, and when he took the final drag from his own cigarette, he blew his white smoke right into the burning grass.

Instead of intermingling into a muted version of each other, the black and white smoke folded into a smoky knot. The contrasting vapors formed pictures the way clouds on a sunny day became dancing hippos or a shark's fin or a bearded man's smile. Except these images were more distinct, one folding into the next like a comic strip told flip-book style.

The pictures told a tale of a love triangle—of a pale boy who falls in love with a radiant goddess, except she only has eyes for an older man who is bright as can be and yet so far away. So she settles for the younger boy, who worships her. He revolves around her, and sometimes he seems to burn as bright in her mind as her real love. Other times, she grows so disinterested in the boy that she can barely see him. He becomes almost invisible to her. The boy knows that he will never fulfill her, and yet he keeps trying. He writes her poems and showers her with gifts. He smothers her. And she secretly pines for that radiant man, though she knows that passion would ultimately consume her.

Rudy looked at his screensaver again—at Heather. "What's the point of love," he said, "if we're not taking risks?"

The voice washed over him again, and this time he wondered if it might sound vaguely feminine—like the kind of gal that had stayed up through many sunrises, had raised many a glass in a smoky bar, and turned many heads upon walking into countless rooms.

"Tell me about her," the voice rippled through him. "Does she, too, shine like the sun?"

He shook his head. "No. No, she doesn't. She's like the boy in your story. She'd give me the world, if I let her."

The voice laughed, and the noise flowed all through his veins, making his heart gallop. The smoke wiggled inside the corners of his eyes. His vision went dark—a thousand shades of dark grey. Somehow, this did not alarm him. He felt safe, cared for. Like a baby in the womb. When the voice spoke again, it flowed over him as if he were a tiny thing stuck inside her mouth clinging to her flexing tongue.

"The world is not hers to give, my friend," she said.

He cleared his throat and said, "I suppose not."

"Do you plan to leave her?"

"I've considered it."

"Because you moon over someone else?"

"Maybe. Or maybe I just need to be alone for awhile. I don't know."

"So why do you keep her picture on your phone?"

He shrugged. "Partly for her. I know what it means to her. But also I like having her there on the screen. It makes me feel like I'm loved."

"But there is another?"

He reached blindly for his cigarettes, tossed another broken one into the direction of the grass, and lit a decent one for himself.

"There's always another," he said. "Her name doesn't matter."

"Because it hurts to say it."

He laughed. "Because it's easier not to. We were lovers for a short while, which is to say I worshipped and she accepted for as long as she could."

"When you're revolving around someone, it's easy to imagine that your partner is dancing with you."

"Yeah, like the trees along this path. If I ride fast enough, it looks like they're twirling."

"If you're going that fast, you best be looking at the trail, not the trees."

He took a drag. "I feel like everything in this discussion is a metaphor for another metaphor."

"Welcome to my life," the voice said.

"Life? I assumed you were a ghost."

"Really?"

"Yeah. Like the ghost of some lady stuck in a love triangle, and you fell along this path and broke your neck. And now near sunset, the ground smolders and up you come, anxious to reconnect with the living. Am I right?"

"Only by the very smallest degree. I am stuck in a love triangle of sorts, but I assure you—despite your species' industrious efforts— I am still very much alive."

"My species? Are you an alien?"

The voice laughed through him, tickling the marrow in his bones. He went lightheaded for a moment, brain squirming in his skull. Sweat dripped down the insides of his shirt.

"I could not possibly be any less alien," she said.

For a moment, the smoke cleared. The sun had set. A half moon hung in the sky behind a veil of black smoke. The bloated crescent gazed down upon them—at once ancient yet refreshingly new and vital. The moon was eternally young, constantly reborn by the rhythm of its cycle. The moon was the boy from the story, he realized.

"Wait," he said. "If the moon is the boy, then that makes you . . ."

The smoke slid back over his eyes. "The Earth, yes."

"I'm having a cigarette with the Earth? Like with a capital E?"

"Well, a wise man once said that every alien civilization calls its planet Earth. So I'm not unique in that regard."

"Why are *you* talking to me?"

"Why do *you* wish upon a star?"

"Um, because they're huge and magnificent and so very beautiful and distant."

"When you're as big as I am, sometimes you have to look down to see the stars. You are my constellations—your rapid movements and constant shuffling. I actually envy the speed with which your lives progress. You can live a life in the time it takes me to make a decision. You're my freckles. My tattoos."

"But tattoos last forever," he said. "We don't."

"Tattoos are just scars, and scars always fade. Nothing lasts forever."

"More metaphors," he said. "It's like we're talking in pictures. So you're really planet Earth? Mother Earth?"

She laughed through him. His toes curled. His belly somersaulted against his spine. He nearly fell over. Comets tails sprinkled across his vision. He was no longer on the trail. He was no longer anywhere, except folded up inside that whispering smoke.

"Believe me when I say that I'm no mother," she said. "I only told you the story in terms that would be most understandable. The moon is no boy, I am no girl, and the sun is no man. In truth, I am at once man and woman and everything in between and beyond. I am at once day and night, autumn and spring—depending which way I'm facing."

"So you're all that, and yet you're still not above this love stuff, huh?"

"Silly boy," she said. "Haven't you heard? Love is what makes the world go round. All clichés are based on some truth. In this case, that truth is quite literal."

He considered her words—who he was talking to. "I'm sorry for all the damage we've done to you—all the pollution and mining and deforesting. It's pretty shitty."

She sighed through him. "You're only hurting yourselves. I'm just surprised you haven't figured that out yet. Trust me. I'll be here long after you're all gone."

"Yeah, I guess you're not going anywhere, huh?"

"That remains to be seen. If I decide to move, you'll know it. Everyone will know it."

Her comment seemed ominous but he pressed onward. "Was the world better before we came along?"

"I was younger then," she said. "It's hard to say. I do miss the Great Auks. They had the most charming proportions."

"What's a Great Auk?"

"It was a bird—like something out of an outlandish daydream. They were tall with beaks as big as their heads. They had these silly little wings—too small to allow them to fly but they swam with such grace. Unfortunately, that left them vulnerable as all hell to your people on land. You hunted them to extinction for their feathers. Fishermen killed the last couple on Eldey Island. The two birds had an egg, but one of the fishermen trampled over it. I felt that egg crack. I felt it in my fiery core. Those fuckers."

The curse word felt like an icy hammer slammed against his brain.

He shivered skinless in the smoky curtain. "The Earth just dropped an F-bomb. Wow."

"Everything begins and ends with a painful break," she said. "The moon's always smiling, but it's so hollow. I know when his light is turned away from me, he's really weeping. Even when he's not there—when he's dark—he's always there. He haunts me the same way I haunt the sun."

"That's his job, right? He's a moon."

She made a tsk-ing noise that sent a jolt down his spine. "I suppose. We're all revolving around something, more or less. None of us are free. It's how the world keeps turning, only . . . only sometimes I grow weary. Sometimes I just want to be still or better yet leave all of this behind. These dancing trees that seem to revolve around you. In reality they are a prison. They make it seem as though they protect you, but in reality they're herding you along. They're hunting you. And whatever pure beautiful unborn part of you might someday be free, they will surely smash under their dirty boots and leave it to rot in the sun."

His head reeled in the smoke. He saw moons washing up on forgotten shores—a storm of feathers and blood. Egg shells cracking. Sparks flying. Everything expanded and regressed into layers of itself. Everything was a shell and nothing was hollow.

"Why are you telling me all of this?" he said.

"So that one day you'll understand."

His phone rang. It was Heather's ringtone—*SexyBack* by Justin Timberlake.

He fell backward out of the smoke and his head smacked against the asphalt. Stars blurred across this vision. *Sexyback* played onward. He waited for the world to refocus but it didn't. It couldn't. Smoke covered everything, ushered now by roaring flames on either side of the path. He sat up and coughed. The smoke twirled around him, a flock of awkward flightless ghosts with stubby wings swimming through the charred air. He crawled blindly down the path, hoping he was going the right direction. Hot asphalt burned his palms and knees. His wounds screamed at the heat. Nearby, a burning tree collapsed. Was the whole world on fire?

At last, the cell phone shut up. His outstretched hand found the greasy gears of his bike, now as hot as fresh coffee. He took a breath, coughed, inhaled again, and righted the bike. He knew he shouldn't be able to breath—not amongst all this churning smoke. Maybe it was some side effect of his time talking with the Earth.

He hoisted onto his bike seat and pedaled blindly through the smoke, which all but eclipsed the trail below his tires. His only means of navigation was the burning trees on either side of the path. He stayed between the fire. Why the hell had he forgotten his helmet at work? His legs pumped at the pedals, so fast that the burning trees did indeed seem to twirl around him.

The smoke raged. The trees danced. Far behind him, Timberlake's *SexyBack* started up again. If he got out of this, he swore to himself that he would break up with Heather and start a new life.

He coughed and pedaled, coughed and pedaled. The rubber grips of his handlebar melted around his fingers, forming gooey half-gloves that seared his already burnt palms. The smoke raked at his eyes, so that finally he had to clench them tight—navigating now only by the sound of the flames and the pulsing beep of the synthesized *SexyBack*.

That was how he was introduced to over 5.7 million people across the world.

At least, that's how many hits the 37-second YouTube video had two weeks later.

Rudy went viral.

Some asshole with a smartphone recorded a clip of his unlikely egress from the raging forest inferno. The video starts with an overview of burning forest and the firemen hooking up to a hydrant. Someone off camera yells, "What the fuck is that?" The camera shifts to the bike path engulfed in flames. From the fiery inferno, Rudy emerges perched upon his bike—all of his hair singed off, hands fused to his handlebars, and his clothes mostly burned away. His legs work furiously at the pedals. He hunches down low like a bird taking flight. His elbows flare out like stubby wings. The crowd cheers as Rudy pedals blindly right into the side of a fire engine. Thankfully the side compartment is open, and a length of hose hangs downward. He slams into the hose, and someone off-camera says, "That was awesome."

If you listened closely over the roar of the flames and the blaring sirens right before Rudy hit the fire engine, you could hear him screaming, ". . . bringing sexy back!" No surprise that one of the more popular copies of the video featured a mix of that very same song.

The paramedics took him to the hospital with broken burns and miraculously only second degree burns.

He woke two days later in a world of hurt. Everything ached. Heather was beside him, holding his forearm because his hands were wrapped in bandages. They were alone in a hospital room. Something beeped and whirred behind him. It was now or never. Time for the big break.

"It's over," is what he wanted to tell her, but a tube was jammed down his throat.

"Oh my god, you're awake," she said, tears glistening in her beautiful sad eyes. "I knew you'd come through, baby."

She never left his side in the hospital. Like a trooper, she managed his family's visits, knowing how much they all aggravated him. His room soon filled with flowers—gifts from people he hadn't heard from in years or didn't even recognize. He didn't yet know he was a mild celebrity. It was his nephew who showed him *The Burning Cycle* video on his smartphone.

Everyone asked the same thing: "How the hell did that happen?"

He always offered the same lie: "I honestly don't remember."

Somehow, he knew that "I was having a cigarette with the Earth because, y'know, she just needed a moment" wasn't going to fly.

The only one who never asked how it happened was Heather, and he suspected it was because she knew she didn't want to know. On his last night in the hospital—after she gave him an impromptu tuggie and was wiping off her hands, he told her the truth.

"The ground along the path was smoking," he said. "I fell off my bike and I sat by the smoldering grass and had a cigarette with the Earth." He coughed. "The Earth actually spoke to me then. She told me that the moon was in love with her, but that she only had eyes for the sun. She told me so many things."

"She did," Heather said, and it didn't sound like a question—more like an affirmation.

"She did." He nodded. "She said the love makes the world go round and that she'd only lose herself in the sun."

"Why'd she tell you all of this?"

He laughed. "I asked her the same question. She said so that some day I'd understand."

"Do you?" she said, as she tucked his limp cock back into his hospital gown.

"I don't think so. Not yet."

The words hid behind his lips: *It's over.*

He couldn't bring himself to say it, not after these past few days in the hospital. She'd been so perfectly helpful and caring. So instead he shared with her something else the Earth had told him.

"Everything begins and ends with a painful break," he said.

She squeezed his thigh. "I guess so."

Life went on.

He made a tidy bit of money working the talk show circuit and doing interviews and being a local celebrity. The extra cash more than made up for the time Heather had missed at work. Later he had a brief endorsement deal from a chain of barbeque restaurants.

Heather had their one and only child almost nine months after the filming of *The Burning Cycle*. They married during the second trimester. The newlyweds named their daughter Terra, since it meant "Earth." If she'd been a boy, they would've called him Justin. Rudy immersed himself in parenting. He found each new year more and more rewarding—the snuggly rooting of the infant years, the amazing growth of the toddler years, the curiosity of the preschool years, the burgeoning energy of the elementary school years, the frenetic pace of the middle school years, and the bittersweet distance of the high school years.

Almost every day, he rode his bike along the bike paths, hoping to see a hint of smoke. He never did.

Almost every evening, he walked and watched the sky, expecting to see the moon suddenly grow more distant. He never did.

Aside from a stubborn knee joint and some scarring, the incident on the bike path left him with little permanent damage—at least not physically. Most nights he had vivid dreams about a beautiful woman and her two love interests—a tanned older man and a pale younger man. Sometimes the dreams were like soap operas. Other times, they were full-on slasher movies or even pornos. The genre varied with the lunar cycle, which meant his dream cycle was in synch with Heather's menstrual cycle. When he woke up screaming, she was plagued by cramps. When he woke with a raging erection, she was frisky as an alley cat.

Still, he wasn't entirely happy. Something was missing. Hollow. Several times a year, he almost told Heather, "It's over."

Yet he could never bring himself to do it.

Some force held them together, be it the steady gravity of their mortgage, the sticky glue of their belongings, or the joyous bonding of their child. By the time the mortgage was paid off and Terra was away at college, he just didn't have the energy to leave. Sometimes he thought about the other woman. He stalked her halfheartedly on social media but never seriously. Whenever he thought of being with her, he remembered that Greek myth about Icarus, the guy who has feathers glued to his arms with wax and flies too close to the sun.

Spoiler alert: the wax melts.

Everything begins and ends with a painful break.

Now, whenever he thinks about feathers or birds, he remembers the Earth's story about the Great Auk—the same bird that is now tattooed on his calf a few inches below the same knee that he'd scraped in the incident. He and Terra visited the tattoo parlor when she graduated from college. A cute girl with a lip ring and blue hair did their tattoos. Terra got a flaming skeleton on a bicycle inked on her ankle. He got a Great Auk, except on his tattoo the bird was flying.

He leans down now on the lawn mower and flexes his calf.

The jaunty bird—now faded and wrinkled—flaps its ridiculously small wings. That trick never ceases to make his grandchildren giggle.

He's sweating. The hot sun bullies his shadow down into the freshly cut grass and yet a chill passes over him. His shadow shifts and shrinks. His mower rumbles beneath him—sloshing his beer—and at first he thinks the plastic hunk of junk might be on the fritz again.

In the house, Heather shrieks. He slips off his mower, and the solar-powered engine immediately cuts off. He limps toward the house, slow without his cane. His wife meets him at the backdoor, face wrinkled and hair grey.

She points up at the sky. "It was on the Cable-less," she says. "Some kind of massive earthquake in China."

Everything begins and ends with a painful break.

He looks up.

The sun is shrinking. Where normally it's the size of a nickel, it's now barely a penny. She holds him tight. He shakes his head and smiles. The Earth finally did it. She found a way to break the cycle.

"What's happening?" she says, her words crystallizing in the air as icy fog. "You're smiling?"

The world lurches and knocks them into the itchy grass. They fall first down and then sideways. In the sky, birds fly in all directions—their internal compasses all out of whack. The sun is no bigger than a dime and it slips from directly above them into the horizon—not into the west over the Lipp's yard where it always falls but to the north past the house. The mower tumbles across the yard.

His hands dig into the grass. Heather's hands grasp him. He

can't not look at the sky, which is now black and full or stars streaming past them. The constellations seem to dance. The moon slides past them. Where normally it's the size of a nickel, it's now the size of a penny. Like a heavy eyelid, its dark side grows. Half full. Dime. Crescent. Gone.

He holds his wife close and whispers with his final breath, "It's over."

The Stink of Animosity

"So, what did she do?"

These are the first words the stranger says to you as he takes the bar stool on your right. The hotel lounge has at least two-dozen seats scattered between the bar and four tables, and only half of those seats are filled. Yet he sits next to you. His voice is almost a growl – all gravel and broken glass – too ragged for someone his age.

Judging from his unblemished skin, you guess the stranger is no more than nineteen or twenty. You search your memories, wondering if he's one of your students at the college. But no, you would remember him. He's got an unkempt, patchy beard and dirty, long hair. Everything about him says wannabe hippie or beatnik: his worn boots, his thrift store brown leather jacket, and his dirty grey t-shirt. His eyes are wild, like he's been chewing on a handful of random pills.

"Who? What are you talking about?" you ask, trying to sound abrupt but not aggressive. You're not looking for a fight. At least, not with him.

"You got the stink of animosity on you, is all. I can smell it; it's so strong. It's not hard to see that you're pissed at someone."

"I'm sure the black eye isn't a clue, is it?" You glance at your reflection in the mirror above the bar – a nice big shiner.

Dangling from the ceiling on thin chains, the dim overhead lamps cast long, swaying shadows that make your eye look worse than it is. From antique speakers, a man's voice croons along with a guitar. The stranger runs his hands through his snow-dusted hair, and you take another sip of your drink. Across the room, a burning log settles in the fireplace with a pop of sparks.

"You hold that glass any tighter, it'll shatter in your hand. In my experience, it takes a woman to get a fella that mad."

"Your experience." You put your glass down. You're ready to go to your hotel room and call it a night. You're in no mood for this conversation, but you need at least one more drink. Why is it you always attract the weird ones?

"I've been in this business a long time, son," says the kid, "long enough to read the anger on your face clear as day."

"And what business is that?" You ignore the fact that this young punk just called you "son."

"Let's just say I help settle problems between people."

The bartender places a beer in front of the stranger, who pulls a crumpled wad of bills out of his pocket and tosses a few dollars on the bar.

"So, what, you're some kind of counselor or mediator or something?"

"Yeah," he says with a bitter chuckle. "I'm a mediator. I mediate people right into the ground." He takes a long drink of his beer, draining nearly half of it.

*

How did you get here?

As a professor of history, this is the central question of your lifetime of study. It's the heart of history, the force behind all inquiry.

In a nightmare, it's the question you never stop to ask yourself. You just accept the context, no matter how bizarre, and move on from there: deeper into the nightmare. If you did ask that simple question, maybe you could unravel the riddle and realize that you're only dreaming. Likewise, when your life becomes a nightmare, it takes you awhile to ask yourself that same question. And by the time you ask, it's likely too late.

Four drinks ago, you stood by your car in the hotel's gravel parking lot, staring at the plume of smoke coming from a crooked chimney. The smoke rose with urgency, a long white snake slithering upward to the bloated, full moon.

Aside from that moon, the only lights were those coming from the hotel's curtained windows, a flicking overhead light at the far end of the lot, and a solitary farmhouse in the distance. Frozen cornfields stretched in all directions, save for a strip of forest that lined this side of the state route and surrounded the hotel premises. The woods were silent; the only noise coming from the hotel's lounge.

It was the kind of Ohio night that would make you pray for darkness. The light of the full moon and the bright blanket of snow combined to reveal too much of everything. You opened your trunk and pulled out your bag. You rummaged through the denim, cotton, and wool until your hands closed on satin.

You pressed the watery fabric to your face and took a deep breath. A sob choked in your throat. Suddenly feeling very foolish, you balled up the satin and tossed it into the trunk. You zipped up the bag and staggered across the parking lot.

*

"Look," you say to the stranger, "I don't mean to be rude, but I'm here to get drunk. I'm not here to talk about my problems."

"Fuck talking about your problem," says the stranger. "I'm talking about ending your problem." He leans in close and whispers, "Permanently."

You take another drink, letting the rum smolder on your tongue before swallowing. "Are you saying you're a… hit man?" you ask, mouthing the last two words.

"Never much cared for that particular term, but yeah, that's what I am – and a damn good one, too."

"Why should I trust you? I don't even know your name." You're only humoring him, of course. Just trying to bring the conversation to a natural conclusion.

"Brenton."

"Brenton?" you echo back.

He nods.

You finish your drink, place it on the bar, and start to get up. "I'm not interested in what you're selling, Brent."

He places a surprisingly strong hand on your shoulder and stares through you with those wild eyes. His fingernails are unclean and long. You size him up. He's younger than you, probably faster. But you're bigger and stronger, and you damn well know how to fight dirty. If it comes to it, you could take him. Of course, that could just be the booze talking.

"The name is Brenton," he says between clenched teeth. "And you're nowhere near drunk enough, friend. Let me buy you another drink. You tell me about your problem, and I'll tell you the solution I can offer. If you're still not interested by the time you finish your drink, then we'll part ways. Deal?"

You're a bit intrigued, but more than that, you're aching for one more drink. You nod and sit down.

"Barkeep," Brenton barks, "another round for my friend and a beer for me." He turns back to you. "You want a whiskey this time? It'd taste better than that stuff you're drinking."

"I'm fine with the rum, thanks."

"Suit yourself," he says, watching the bartender. "All that hard stuff's too strong for me. I'm a beer man."

"Well, wait until you get a little older, Brenton," you say. "You'll develop a taste for it."

Brenton starts laughing at that, a rumble from deep in his gut that sounds like a locomotive engine. He's still chuckling by the time the drinks arrive.

"So, tell me about your problem," he says, after the bartender leaves.

"First, I have a question for you, Mr. Brenton." You're using the tone you use with your students when they make a particularly dumb comment in class. "What the fuck kind of hitman solicits business in a hotel bar? I mean, don't you think you're coming on a little too strong?"

"Son, you ever known a dog that didn't greet you by shoving its nose in your crotch? Well, I've got the same approach – I just cut through all the chit-chat bullshit."

You try hard to block the image of Brenton sniffing your crotch and humping your leg.

"Brenton, you're not a dog."

"Even better," he says. "I'm a goddamn werewolf."

*

How did you get here?

History sure as fuck isn't about learning from our mistakes. That's just the bullshit line you feed to college freshman who think everything they learn has to have a pragmatic purpose. The truth is that history – the understanding of how you got here – is how you connect the world of the living with the ever-expanding world of the dead. It's how you breathe life into the decay all around you.

Just a couple hours ago, the moon was fat and high above you, dressed in gloomy clouds sprinkled with stars. You were on your back atop an Indian mound, lying on the frozen ground. A set of rabbit tracks – frozen Rorschach blots – crossed the mound, only briefly scattered by your own half-assed snow angle. You finished the last of a bottle of rum, enjoying the contrast between the fire in your belly and the frozen skin at your back.

Closing your eyes, you turned your head, pressing one ear against the cold soil – the swollen Earth not unlike a tumor or a pregnant belly. Ignoring the sounds of distant traffic, you listened to the mound's story. Listened so closely that you could almost hear the marching of feet – determined workers building yet another layer onto the mound.

About the same time that the first Olympics were being held in Greece, some poor Adena bastard had died in his home. He'd been buried in the soil beneath his home, and the whole thing had been set ablaze. Soil was then placed lovingly over the ashes.

Over the years, maybe around the time that Buddha was born or the Great Wall of China was being built or the Roman Empire was rising to its height, more Adena died. Their bodies were placed in rectangular pits dug into the same soil, maybe arranged solemnly over planks or logs, and then set on ablaze. And again, the ashes were covered with another layer of soil.

That was how the mound was created, layer by layer, gradually swelling with its stratified tombs. The workers carried coarse baskets bulging with dirt that was soon poured onto the dead remains – some already cremated, others whole.

This is where you took all your dates back in college. You took Andrea here, when you had first joined the faculty and she was a grad student. You remember being so impressed with how unimpressed she was with you. With your mound.

*

You nearly spit out your drink, you laugh so hard. "A werewolf. Well fuck me. What big eyes you have, grandma."

Brenton turns on his barstool so that he's facing you, then motions for you to face him. He leans forward, and for one horrible second you think he's going to kiss you. But his face goes next to you, so that his scraggly beard tickles your cheek. He inhales deeply and then pulls away.

"You were lying on the ground earlier tonight," he says. "In the same spot, a rabbit peed this afternoon. For dinner, you had a hamburger with pickles. You were drinking a different kind of rum earlier. Maybe Captain Morgan's. You don't wash your hands after you pee. You had orange juice this morning for breakfast. You jerked off earlier today – no lubrication. You use an herbal shampoo. You deodorant is Right Guard. You own a cat. No, two cats. They eat dry cat food. You smoked a cigar recently, probably yesterday. Want me to go on?"

"No," you say.

"Fine." He sips his beer and smiles. His teeth are crooked. The two top canine teeth protrude jaggedly from the rest of his teeth. It gives him a beastly, fierce smile. "My, oh my," he says. "What big eyes *you* have."

"You got all that from smelling me?"

He nods and you study his eyes. You've seen that look before: in they eyes of Sean, the crazy student who was kicked out of the University for attacking his roommate. He later was institutionalized after an incident with his family. You were the roommate's advisor, and you remember him telling you how sensitive Sean had been about smells. The attack had started over burning incense.

Clearly, Brenton's crazy, but it's a kind of crazy you can use. Already, a plan is hatching in your head, wiggling out of its shell. *A man has drinks with a stranger in a lounge, tells the stranger his problems. Turns out the stranger is crazy, out of his mind. The man never thought the stranger would go after his wife; he was just venting to the man. He was just getting his problems out in the open.*

"So," says Brenton, "tell me about your problem, and I'll tell you how much it'll cost to bury it."

*

How did you get here?

Let's face it. The world's not getting any younger. We're being smothered under an ancestral tidal wave of memories and memorabilia, while at the same time we're obsessed with being younger, looking younger. The only way to deny that you're well on the way to becoming history: money.

Right around sunset earlier today, you walked into the bank and stood in line. Your eye throbbed so hard it hurt to blink. You rubbed the bridge of your nose, as if you had a headache from the harsh fluorescent lights on the ceiling. But really, you were just holding back the tears.

Finally, the teller greeted you with a frayed smile. You opened your wallet and pulled out your bank card and driver's license.

"I'd like to withdraw four thousand dollars," you said. That was about half of the emergency fund. Well, truthfully a bit more than half.

She took your cards and typed on her keyboard.

"We're taking a vacation. My wife and I. Off-season. It's the best time to travel – lots of discounts. You can save a ton of money."

You didn't know what you were planning to do with the money, other than disappear for awhile, maybe go on a drinking binge or find a hooker. Whatever you were doing and wherever you were going, you figured it'd be places that take cash only.

"How would you like that?" asked the teller.

"Cash."

She sighed, but only barely. "Twenties okay?"

"Oh. Yeah. Sorry. That'd be fine."

*

"My wife's having an affair." The words sting your tongue like hot tea. "She's... she's going to leave me."

"Tough luck," says Brenton, "but really, is that the sort of problem that's worth digesting?"

"We have a son. I have a son. I can't let her take him away from me. And she will. I know she will." Purposefully, you don't tell Brenton your son's name – not a detail he needs to know. You don't want his demented mind gnawing on the name. Tommy.

"So, it's about the pup," says Brenton. "That's reasonable."

"I just can't handle the idea of another man raising my child. Another man being called 'Daddy.' Another man tucking my son into bed. I can't do it. I want this bastard dead."

"I understand," says Brenton with a grunt.

"You have kids?"

He shakes his head. "Not that I know of, though lord knows I've scattered enough seed across this fine country of ours."

"How much?" you finally ask.

"Hard to say. I don't keep a little black book."

"No, I meant how much would it cost? For you to..."

"Kill your wife's lover?" Brenton sits back on his stool and grins. "Eat him up? Bury the scraps? How much you got?"

"Three thousand, minus my bar tab."

"That'll do just fine," he says, arching his eyebrows and licking his lips. You know it's just a combination of booze and imagination, but you could almost swear his pointed teeth are longer.

"How much..." You pause, rubbing your throbbing eye. "How much extra to eat my wife, too?"

*

How did you get here?

The bathroom shower hisses in the next room. Behind a locked door, Andrea is washing herself clean of you.

Her black sweater, white blouse, red satin panties, and grey pants lay on the floor of the bedroom like scattered remains. You kicked and stomped the outfit, and then fell to your knees, crying. You pressed the blouse to your face, blotting gently at the tears. Your eye was already starting to swell.

The blouse smelled like her, a mix of delicate perfume and garden herbs. It occurred to you then that you might never again wake up to that smell. You cried all the harder.

You left the house carrying an overstuffed suitcase and a bottle of Captain Morgan. As you backed the Jaguar out of the driveway, you notice a car parked on the street just a few doors down. On the off chance that the driver is your wife's new lover, you shove a middle finger out the window as you pass by.

*

Brenton chuckles, an untuned engine sputtering. For a moment, you feel as though you have been buried in an avalanche. It's all happening so fast.

"The wife's free," says Brenton. "Because I like you."

You finish your drink and close your eyes. Your voice sounds as if it's coming from your belly. "We live at 724 Honeycomb Court in Kwatokee, just a few miles up the road."

"House numbers and street names only matter in your world," says Brenton, shaking his head, "but not in mine. All I need to track her is a piece of her clothing. I just need the scent – and half the cash. I collect the rest when the job's done."

What the hell… why not? If it'll make him happy, then why not? "I… I've got something of hers in the car."

"It has to be something she wore," he says. "Can't be a purse or a tube of lipstick or some stupid shit like that."

"It's… a pair of panties. She wore them tonight."

Brenton laughs and shakes his head.

*

How did you get here?

"This conversation is over," said Andrea. "Just get your things and leave. I'll pick up Tommy tomorrow morning from the

Andersons. I'll call your cell phone tomorrow night and we can talk. Don't call me."

Your family room was quiet. Your once happy smiling pictures on the wall now sneered at you. The silence between you had a pulse of its own, like when you stick your fingers in your ears. It's not silence, but it's not noise either.

"You think…" You paused, choosing your words like blood-splattered knives. "You think I'm just going to let you take our son away from me, you little bitch? You think I'll let some other man raise my child? Are you out of your mind, you dumb slut?"

You didn't even see it coming.

Her right fist slammed into your eye, knocking you off-balance. You stumbled backward over the end table, which collapsed under your weight.

Her footsteps padded up the stairs.

*

In the parking lot, Brenton takes off his coat and drapes it over his shoulder. The full moon stares down at you, unblinking and bright. Its gaze sparkles across the frozen cornfields in the distance.

"This used to be all trees," says Brenton. "In a few more years, folks will stand out here and talk about how it used to be all cornfields."

"That's…" You fumble for a word. A shame? Sad? You settle on, "…true."

Brenton tilts his head backward, letting the moon shine on his hairy face. "You know what they call the November full moon?"

You shake your head.

"It's the hunter's moon."

Still shaking your head, you walk all the way across the parking lot toward the far side of the hotel.

*

How did you get here?

The whole drive home from the funeral parlor, Andrea talked and you listened. Her words were made of venom and her voice was so cold. After awhile you stopped listening, focusing instead on the road ahead, dwelling instead on phrases like:

...so *quick to anger*...

...*can't take it anymore*...

...*how you manipulate everything*...

...think I don't know about your little grad assistants...
...drinking's gotten out of control...

You tasted the tears in the back of your throat, all salty and warm. The road was a long, grey snake, slithering beneath you. At some point, you parked in the driveway. You sat there shivering in the dark, while Andrea finished speaking.

Her words were spoonfuls of dirt tossed over your chest cavity. And one phrase in particular served as the final epitaph: *I've found someone else.*

*

It's dark and desolate at the back of the lot, where a narrow strip of trees follows a drainage ditch to the rear of the property.

When you reach your grey Jaguar, you pop open the trunk and fumble around in the shadows. The trunk is full of the usual things: a tire iron, road flares, a ratty blanket and a shoebox filled with out-of-date road maps. By the dim light of the trunk light, you find the red satin panties.

Not making eye contact with Brenton, you hand him the panties.

"I don't know why I grabbed these. I guess I... I just..." Words fail you.

Brenton takes the bunch of satin, sniffs it, and stuffs it into his coat pocket. He pats you roughly on the shoulder. "You don't owe me no explanations. I don't have a dog in this fight. Hell, I am the dog in this fight, right?"

*

How did you get here?

You were among the first to leave the viewing. Tears streamed down Andrea's face as you guided her into your car. Going around to the driver's side, you sat beside Andrea in the dark, turning the key in the ignition. The engine rumbled at your feet.

"I'm sorry," you said. "I didn't except you to be this upset. I didn't think you really knew Caroline."

"I didn't," said Andrea. "I just... Sometimes when you're staring death in the face, things become so clear to you. All the time that you've wasted. Death clarifies things."

"Yeah," you said, though you hadn't the faintest notion what she was talking about.

You backed the car out of the parking space, then steered

smoothly out of the funeral home's crowded parking lot.

Only when you're on the street did she say it, and you knew right away that it was trouble. Your heart flinched at her words: "We need to talk."

*

"I knew… I knew the second she put the engagement ring on her finger. I knew it would end badly." A cold tear snuggles and freezes against your cheek. Everything around you feels alien and obscene. Brenton is swaying slightly, either out of boredom or anticipation. A hint of red satin, like a shiny fresh wound, sticks out of his pocket. And finally you ask the big question. "Is it going to hurt?"

"It'll be quick," says Brenton, still looking you in the eye. "Don't worry. I never start eating until after the prey has stopped breathing."

Something inside you snaps, some little invisible membrane behind your heart, and you punch the open trunk lid with five wild jabs. The car grunts in return; the lid wobbles. For the second time today, tears spill freely down your cheeks.

Brenton watches calmly until you are finished, then hands you a handkerchief. You notice with a chill that his eyes have lost their wild, frayed appearance. By the light of the moon, his eyes look steady and calm; twin fires that could burn forever. The hair on his hands is longer, probably a trick of the moonlight.

You use the handkerchief first to wipe away your tears, and then to wipe the blood of your knuckles. The cold bites into the wounds with a sobering kiss.

"Thanks, Brenton."

"Don't mention it." There's a low growl in his voice.

Still holding the handkerchief, you hold your hands under the lights in the trunk. Your knuckles are torn and raw. Good. You can tell the police that you argued with Brenton, that he had suddenly gotten irate and confused. That it came to blows and you fought with him.

You fold your hands into fists, and that's when you notice your own initials on Brenton's handkerchief.

*

How did you get here?
The funeral home made you shiver. It had that queer smell of

flowers soaked in chemicals. There was already a good-sized crowd, mostly other professors from the college. You put an arm around Andrea's waist and walked down the aisle.

The portion of the rug in front of the casket was well-worn, a reminder of just how many people had made this walk before you. Of just how many souls had made that final walk before Caroline. It made death seem cheap and common.

The woman in the casket was hardly recognizable. Her flesh was rubbery and pasty, ready to slide off her skull. Her hands were as delicate as rice paper. A few snippets of conversation managed to wiggle free from the droning of the crowd:

"…that time she put that poster on her door…"

"…wonder what happens to that nice desk in her office…"

"…to see Albert looks okay. The poor…"

You felt Andrea shaking next to you, and your first thought was that she was laughing. You pulled her tightly to you at the waist, and stared into her eyes. Tears were streaming down her cheeks and rounding the curve at her jawline. She looked at you with imploring eyes, and you handed her a monogrammed handkerchief.

*

"This is my handkerchief," you say to Brenton, stupidly, as if he had it by mistake. Only after the words leave your lips do you understand what the handkerchief means.

I just need the scent...

As if on cue, the moon peeks from behind a cloud, as wide-eyed as a child peeking on his parents having sex. This metaphor disturbs you; you'd always thought of the moon as an elder, not as a child.

Brenton grins, revealing canine teeth that have now protruded well past his other teeth. The hair on his face has grown longer, covering all but his eyes, nose and mouth. His nails have slid forward and curved into sharp points. He's breathing heavy, almost panting, and his eyes glow a soft yellow.

You're suddenly aware of the wad of cash in your pocket.

…and half the cash. I collect the rest when the job's done.

You realize that the cash isn't the down payment; it's the balance owed.

"Sometimes it's better if you run," he says, the words barely recognizable – think of words shredded with a cheese grater and then rubbed between two pieces of sandpaper. "It's better if you don't see it coming."

You look around frantically, weighing your options. He's standing between you and the hotel, so your only choice is to dash into the trees and double back to the hotel. Taking a deep breath, you grab the tire iron and throw it at Brenton.

Not bothering to see whether or not it hit him, you sprint into the narrow strip of woods. Behind you, you hear a grunt and the clang of metal. The bushes slash at your skin as you enter the little woods.

*

How did you get here?

Andrea talked for a few moments to Mrs. Anderson on their front porch. What's her name – Sally? Sylvia? Tommy waved at you with a grin, and dashed past Mrs. Anderson, eager to play with Randy. Honestly, who names a kid Randy? Randy Anderson?

Tommy's hair was typically askew, shining in the fading daylight. Already, the hint of muscle played against his chest. Day by day, he was less a boy and more a man. Your son. Your legacy. Your living history.

Andrea walked back to the car, hands crossed over her ample breasts, shrouded in a tight black sweater. She smiled weakly at you as she crouched to get into the Jag. You backed out of the driveway, patting her on the knee.

She began to talk about the Andersons, about the weekend ahead, and so on. Honestly, you weren't even paying attention.

*

The ground is frozen and unforgiving, causing you to stumble and flail between the trees. All you can hear is the sound of your own gasping breath and heavy footsteps. Blood pounds a jarring rhythm in your ears. Legs aching, you emerge on the other side the woods. Across a frozen cornfield, the lights of the farmhouse twinkle in the distance. It seems like a better option than doubling back through the woods. You sprint across the uneven ground.

You don't even see him coming.

Something heavy hits your back and you thud to the frozen ground face-first. Hot breath flushes over the back of your neck, followed by intense pressure. Something under your skull snaps and tears. You go limp.

Brenton rolls you onto your back with a gentle nudge of his foot, which is now bare, hairy, and clawed. He's shirtless, and his chest is covered with a thick carpet of hair.

He kneels next to you, as if praying. Placing one clawed hand over your heart and the other over your thigh, his head hovers over your stomach, and for one idiotic moment you wonder if he's going to give you a blowjob. Without ceremony, he bites into your stomach, gnawing at the flesh, pulling it away from the ribs. You try to scream, but all that comes out is a sickly whine – not even enough to smother the sound of his chewing.

He shudders every time he swallows, and you remember an off-hand remark he'd made about not liking the taste of rum.

Oddly, the worst part isn't the pain. Be it the shock or the cold, the pain eventually fades. No, the worst part is the feeling of his teeth scraping against your bones. It makes you feel like a garden, like a freshly dug grave.

And just like that – you're history. Steam pours out of your torn stomach, an ancient snake ready to swallow the silly, childish moon.

About the Author

Rob E. Boley grew up in Enon, Ohio, a little town with a big Indian mound. He later earned a B.A. and M.A. in English from Wright State University in Dayton, Ohio. He's the author of *The Scary Tales* series of dark fantasy novels featuring mash-ups of classic fairy tale characters and horror monsters. His fiction has appeared in several markets, including *A cappella Zoo, Pseudopod, Clackamas Literary Review, Intersections: Six Tales of Ouija Horror,* and *Best New Werewolf Tales.* He lives with his daughter in Dayton, where he works for his alma mater. Each morning and most nights, he enjoys making blank pages darker.

Get to know Rob better:

www.robboley.com
Twitter: @robboley
Facebook.com/RobBoleyAuthor
Email: rob@robboley.com

Howling Unicorn Press

Howling Unicorn Press is the lovechild of authors Rob E. Boley and Megan Hart, who, writing together as E. E. March, plan to conjure stories that thrill, chill, and fulfill.

Also by Howling Unicorn Press--

Intersections: Six Tales of Ouija Horror
Little Secrets by Megan Hart
Womb: Six Tales of Maternal Mayhem by Megan Hart

Look for more coming from Howling Unicorn Press in the future and stay up to date at:

www.howlingunicornpress.com
www.facebook.com/HowlingUnicornPress

Drop us a line at:
howlingunicornpress@gmail.com

www.ingramcontent.com/pod-product-compliance
Lightning Source LLC
Chambersburg PA
CBHW051513170626
46811CB00002B/803